W9-BVO-115
3 5674 00684601 9

THE TRUXTON CIPHER

A Simon and Schuster Novel of Suspense

Henry Gruppe

SIMON AND SCHUSTER NEW YORK

c,1

S

Published by Simon and Schuster
Rockefeller Center, 630 Fifth Avenue
New York, New York 10020
SBN 671-21573-6
Library of Congress Catalog Card Number: 73-8027
Designed by Jack Jaget
Manufactured in the United States of America

1 2 3 4 5 6 7 8 9 10

Tell our mother Sparta,
stranger who passes by,
that faithful to her law
we lie below.

—Epitaph for Leonidas and
the Spartans of Thermopylae

In important cases, where the facts are various and complicated, where there appears to be ground for suspecting criminality, or where crime has been committed, or much blame incurred without any certainty on whom it ought chiefly to fall, a court of inquiry affords the best means of collecting, sifting, and methodizing information for the purpose of enabling the convening authority to decide upon the necessity and expediency of further judicial proceedings.

—Article 1718, U.S. Navy Regulations

BLOCK ISLAND SOUND, 1972

One

"Hey, Chief, look here!"

The apprentice radarman, his face tinted an eerie green in the loom of battle-lit electronic equipment, grease-penciled in the third *X*. Using parallel rulers, he drew a line through the three marks, the line plunging straight through the center of his radar screen.

The aircraft carrier's Chief Radarman sauntered over and studied the picture for a moment. "What's the trouble?"

"That destroyer to the south of us, the one going to plane-guard station. I have her on collision course."

The Chief smiled tolerantly. "They all start like that when they turn out of formation. Gets them back in a hurry and impresses the brass. You don't think he'd be dumb enough to run into us, do you?"

Indeed, there seemed no cause for alarm. The aircraft carrier *Argonne* was forging east through a flat sea with two destroyers. The formation was on a routine night operation, the carrier preparing to launch aircraft through the gentle mist that fell upon them. Visibility was good, but the mist was a nuisance. Up on the bridge a few moments earlier, they had discussed the matter.

"Still okay to launch?" The carrier's Executive Officer held up open palms to indicate the softly falling moisture.

"Neither snow, nor rain, nor gloom of night . . . sure it's okay," the Air Operations Officer said. He leaned over the wet bridge coaming and checked the flight deck, where the bridles of steam catapults were being attached to Flight One aircraft. "Ready in five minutes," he estimated.

At moments like this the Exec was satisfied to be old and just ship's company, thereby ineligible for the hundred-mile-an-hour jolt that would enable the pilots to claw wildly upward through blackness. "Airedales ready in five," he reported to his Commanding Officer. "Wind seems to be coming from the south. Radar reports negative shipping down that way on the twenty-mile scale."

Argonne's Captain considered the matter thoughtfully. While this was a routine mission, any night launch was still a tricky business. He wanted every precaution taken. He looked south and east, where his two destroyers, each a mile and a half away, screened him from the "hostile" submarine that was to "attack" him during this training exercise. One of those vessels should be astern of the carrier in case an aircraft flamed out and went into the sea during launch. "Very well," he finally said. "Assign a plane guard."

"Aye, sir." The Exec consulted the Operation Order. "*Somerset* has the duty." With a wave of his hand, he indicated the red lights on the horizon to the south of them.

"As you wish. Order her into position."

The Executive Officer himself sent the signal over voice radio. He heard the answering "Roger, out" from the destroyer, and by the time he regained the bridge rail, the red lights had already begun to shift position as the destroyer turned toward them. The carrier hurtled through darkness for another long minute before the Exec asked, "Permission to turn south, sir?" The enormous carrier took three times as long to turn as her dashing consorts. If orchestrated properly, everyone wound up in his new position at the same time.

"Very well."

In the gleaming wheelhouse of *Argonne* the helmsman spun the wheel, and far below them the carrier's enormous rudder moved ponderously to starboard. The Executive Officer used voice radio to tell the destroyer what he was doing.

Seconds ticked away. Now the carrier and her plane guard, *Somerset,* were racing toward each other on reciprocal courses, spanning the mile and a half at a rate of close to seventy miles an hour. The Exec could see the green and red running lights of the destroyer and the phosphorescence that flashed amid the ghostly white waves under her stem. Sometimes in this maneuver the destroyer approached the carrier with the caution of a porcupine intent on making love to his girlfriend, but not this destroyer. She was coming on strong.

"Eager beaver," the Exec observed to his Commanding Officer.

Argonne's Captain grunted. Small boys stay out of the way of big boys is the *modus operandi* of any naval formation. His concern was internal, and he was now worried about the cant of his flight deck, on which rested so many costly aircraft. "Better ease your rudder, Number One," he cautioned the Exec. He glanced up at the onrushing destroyer. "He's close, but he'll come right in a moment and drop into position all puffy and pleased with himself. I know these daredevils."

They could see the destroyer clearly now, her bridge and upperworks oddly devoid of crewmen. Driven by an unseen hand, she bore down upon them like the *Flying Dutchman.* Sparks flew from her funnels, and white water streamed from her hissing stem. The Exec didn't relax until he saw the gap between the destroyer's funnels begin to widen as she started into the long, graceful turn. A second later, he froze in horror. The destroyer was turning the wrong way—toward the carrier's bow and not away.

Suddenly all was confusion, the orderly routine of the carrier's wheelhouse completely destroyed. The Exec swung the engine-room-annunciator handles to ALL BACK FULL. Groping for the collision-alarm handle, he heard the Captain order, "Left hard rudder." With the *whoop-whoop* of the collision alarm wailing about him, the Exec ran to the bridge wing and pointed to the destroyer, as though he were Merlin and could make the little vessel disappear. In a sense, the destroyer did disappear—partially, at least. A good portion of *Somerset* was passing under the enormous overhang of the flight deck. His knees suddenly weak and trembling, the Exec clung to the bridge coaming, hoping against hope. Then he heard the first awful shriek of metal against metal. "Oh, my God!" he softly moaned.

Two

CONFIDENTIAL

PRECEDENCE:	IMMEDIATE
INDICATOR:	041012 ZULU
FROM:	CHIEF NAVAL OPERATIONS
TO:	COMDESLANT TG 94.1.2
	COMAIRLANT
	COMSUBFLOT ONE
	JAG
	CONAVHOSPITALNEWPORT

PART ONE OF TWO X IRONSTRIKE EXERCISE TERMINATED EFFECTIVE RECEIPT THIS MSG X SPIKEFISH DETACHED PROCEED AS DIRECTED COMSUBFLOT ONE X REMAINDER TASK FORCE PROCEED NARRAGANSETT AREA X PICKERING ASSIST ARGONNE AS REQUIRED X

PART TWO OF TWO X COMDESLANT ORDERED CONVENE COURT INQUIRY USING AUTHORITY NAVREGS ARTICLE 1718 X JAG TO NOMINATE TRIAL COUNSEL X REPRESENTATION COMAIRLANT REQUESTED X FOR ARGONNE X REQUEST FULL REPORT DAMAGE

SUSTAINED X AIRLIFT SOMERSET SURVIVORS TO QUONSET FIRST LIGHT X FOR CO NAVHOSPITALNEWPORT X PROVIDE MEDICAL ASSISTANCE AS REQUIRED X FOR COMDESLANT X COMAIRLANT X JAG X ADVISE NOMINEES COURT INQUIRY TO CNO BY CLOSE BUSINESS TODAY LATEST X

CONFIDENTIAL

"You were there, Chief. You saw it. *His* fault! He killed them all." His leg in a spotless cast, the young lieutenant groaned with pain as the small plane banked sharply. Shortly after daylight, the battered *Argonne* had turned into the wind again, this time to launch an S2A carrying ashore the first of *Somerset*'s few survivors. A large oil slick undulating west of Block Island marked the last remains of the sunken destroyer. The pilot, his curiosity satisfied, rolled the aircraft out of its turn, and they then thrummed steadily north through gray clouds toward the Quonset Point Naval Air Station.

"I don't know nothing, Mr. Tolley." The Chief Quartermaster's hands were swathed in thick, bloodstained bandages, his face twisted with pain. He had to yell over the noise of the engines in order to be heard by the young lieutenant who sat next to him.

"But you were there. You saw it all."

"Let the court of inquiry sort it out. Let the Navy decide," the Chief urged. "I just feel sorry for him."

"I don't. He's been trouble ever since he joined the ship."

"Careful, Mr. Tolley. Ain't no time for wild statements."

"That's okay for you to say, Chief. Your leg isn't broken. That bastard up there will pay. I swear it. He'll swing for this."

The subject of this discussion, the ill-fated destroyer's Executive Officer, Lieutenant Commander Harry St. John, slumped in the copilot's chair on the flight deck of the small aircraft. Perhaps because he was aware of the sentiments then being expressed behind him, St. John's expression reflected little happiness, considering the fact that he was still alive and returning home.

Of thirteen officers assigned to the destroyer, Harry had been the Officer of the Deck at the moment of collision—the man responsible for the last movements of the destroyer. Over six feet in height and of muscular build, he slouched in the small, worn leather seat, torn between anguish and an enormous fatigue. He studied the spreading oil on the water below with soft Irish-green eyes, red-lined with fatigue. His expression was that of a man who had stared at Hell and still had the Devil to face.

Once departure had been taken from Block Island, the small plane traversed the remaining distance to the mainland within a short interval. The pilot picked up a wing tip's distance from the crash truck and throttled back. The horn sounded, unexpected and harsh, as the wheels went down. They flared out over the tarmac, and with one gentle bump the men from the destroyer were back home.

A short, chubby naval officer known to Harry St. John as "Pozo" King was waiting at the foot of the debarkation ladder. Flashbulbs exploded, and microphones were thrust before their faces. Over the snarl of the idling propellers and the tumult of the press, Commander King shouted to him through the megaphone of his hands, ". . . appointed recorder at the inquiry."

"Say again!"

Before he could reply, King was forcibly separated from St. John by shouting newsmen. "Your story . . . first thoughts as the collision occurred . . . how you escaped uninjured . . ."

Grim-faced, Harry forced his way through to the waiting ambulance. Like a flock of starlings, the disappointed reporters darted back toward the other passengers.

The last two obstacles in St. John's path were a small, dapper man with shiny, pointed shoes and a lumbering young fellow dressed in a torn mackinaw and filthy headband. "If you'll sign this, we'll see that your civil rights are protected," the dapper man suggested with a faint smile, at the same time proffering an inexpensive ball-point pen and a typewritten statement. Harry plucked the paper from the man's fingers. The statement he was being asked to sign denounced the military-industrial complex, the war in Vietnam, Polaris submarine patrols, and the inhuman lot of the American seaman. Harry tore the paper into neat quarters and tossed the pieces to the ground. Then he stepped hard and purposely on the shiny shoes of the dapper man.

Despite this affront, the man continued to smile. He nodded briefly to his bearded companion, who produced a pair of handcuffs and proceeded to chain himself to the door handle of the ambulance. Shouting, "Murderers! Murderers!" at the top of his lungs, the youth emptied a flagon of red paint over the back of the vehicle. The press hesitated only a moment and then pounced. This was better than a trio of shipwrecked sailors. This was real news.

St. John and King vaulted into the ambulance as the cameras swung in their direction. Before they could draw the blinds, film recorded the two officers staring with distaste at the antics of the young man attached outside while his associate produced further papers with a flourish.

"My client," he explained while hurriedly distributing the leaflets, "wishes to exercise his right of free expression by denouncing the military-industrial complex of this country . . ." He had started on the Seventh Fleet by the time the shore patrol led him away. The press meticulously recorded every gesture.

Finally, the ambulance was maneuvered into an empty hangar, the young man trotting behind it and finding it somewhat difficult to run and orate at the same time. In the comparative silence of the hangar, Pozo King explained his presence:

"Ops Twenty was asked to furnish a recorder at the

inquiry, and I was appointed. I'll need your statement." Pozo's office, Operations Twenty, a small unit directly under the Chief of Naval Operations, was responsible for global destroyer operations.

Harry extracted from a pocket the two pages he had dictated to *Argonne*'s yeoman that morning. He inquired, "Who's on the court?" Before replying, Pozo ran a quick eye over the summary of events as Harry had briefly portrayed them.

"Uh . . . it's a pretty good makeup, we think. Two captains from DesLant: Peter Lord and Davy MacDonald. J.A.G. is furnishing Jack Hawk, and ComAirLant sent along Ed Burnside."

DesLant was Headquarters, Destroyers Atlantic; J.A.G. was the Judge Advocate General; ComAirLant was Commander, Naval Air Atlantic.

"Look here, Harry," Pozo demanded; "is this all?"

"Is *what* all?"

"Your statement, I mean, surely you can say more than this?"

"I may, but not for now. Is Hawk that bright-ass lawyer who wrote the book on naval disasters?"

"Yes. I think so, at least."

"I see. Did Hawk ever have a command of his own?"

"Not to my knowledge."

"They never do, do they?"

"Harry, Hawk's going to throw the book at you!"

"Let him."

"Harry, you don't seem to understand. You could get twenty years."

"I'm alive. Last night I didn't think I would be."

"You may wish you hadn't escaped when all this is over."

While St. John digested this cheerless observation, the remainder of the party joined them. Pozo looked at Harry several times and shook his head, but he managed to remain silent during the long ride back to Aquidneck

Island. They arrived at the Newport Base Hospital ninety minutes later. The survivors were issued pajamas, sedated, and assigned private rooms. Having attended to any urgent medical problems, *Argonne*'s doctors had decided that what the men needed most was rest.

"Pozo, one last thing before you go," Harry requested. "Get in touch with Lieutenant Halliday at Base Operations and tell her I'd like to see her tonight."

"Sure, Harry. Go ahead, sleep it off. When you come around, I hope you'll be a little more cooperative."

Harry smiled sadly. "What you want is what I'm trying to forget."

The sign stated clearly that the area she was entering was off limits to nonhospital personnel, but Diane Halliday strode through the entranceway so briskly, with a manner so forthright and an expression so determined, that even the senior nurse monitoring the corridor thought twice about making an issue of this affront to administrative regulations.

Lieutenant Halliday was a tall blond girl, slim as a wand, and the possessor of a figure that made even the sensibly tailored WAVE uniform she wore appear stylish. It was her hair—cut in short, mannish fashion—the absence of make-up, and a firm no-nonsense manner that had inspired the boys in the operations center to christen her "Ironpants." But if one looked twice, the hair was a shining honey blond, and the smooth, creamy skin needed no improvement.

When she finally found Harry's room, she paused for a moment to erase any hint of concern from her expression. Then she pushed open the door and went in.

Harry had awakened at twilight. The sedative had temporarily fogged his memory of the previous night, and his sleep had been deep and untroubled. Propping himself up in bed, he surveyed his new environment.

Flickering pink sunshine warmed the spartan, chrome-and-Naugahyde-furnished hospital room. His few belongings were folded neatly upon a small dresser. His worldly cares were for the moment reduced to this small, utilitarian cubicle. He stretched and drew animal pleasure from the feeling of a physical being that was both strong and capable. It was good to be alive, no matter how uncertain the future. He was searching for a cigarette when the door opened.

Leaning back on the doorknob, Diane paused and regarded him with a cynical half smile. Finally she asked, "Harry, Harry, what am I going to do with you?"

"Well, for openers you can come over here."

"You're hurt?"

"Come here and I'll show you."

She correctly read his intent. "There are corpsmen all over the place."

"And I almost got killed last night. One puts a premium on time after that kind of experience."

"Well, we are going to waste a lot more before I climb into bed with you here."

"Diane," he begged.

"Oh, Harry." She walked across to the bed.

He half rose and pulled her to him. Her fine blond hair fell against his face. Her long eyelashes brushed his cheek. Hungrily his mouth closed on hers while his hand fumbled with the buttons of her blouse. She moaned softly, and he felt her nipple harden. Then, quite suddenly, she stiffened and pushed away.

"No! It's always the same with us," she complained. "And I was worried."

She slipped from his grasp just as the door burst open and a young, fat corpsman backed into the room juggling a tray of food.

"Chow down, Commander," the boy announced with the

breezy impertinence of all male nurses. He set the tray on Harry's bed, not failing to note Diane's open blouse.

The meal was an institutional nightmare: canned juice, fried chicken, mashed potatoes, canned peas, and fruit cup. As hungry as he was, Harry shuddered.

"Thanks. I'll ring when I'm finished."

"Anything you want, Commander, you just give me a tinkle on the phone there and let me know," the corpsman offered, ogling Diane.

"Yeah, I'll give you a tinkle."

When they were alone again, Diane asked, "You don't think he was spying on us?"

"Oh, hell no," Harry lied. "Even if he did, it wouldn't matter. This afternoon he told me a rather pathetic story about a couple that used to screw every time she came to visit him. Finally, the hospital staff became so outraged they restricted her visits to the lounge on the ground floor. The first time they met there, they dropped from sight within moments. Twenty minutes later, the head witch doctor found them tangled up in the phone booth. The booth had to be cut apart in order to get them out without castrating him. The nurses are still talking about it."

Her smile held a hint of prim disapproval. After a minute, she sat on the edge of the bed and began to feed him pieces of chicken. Gravely he studied her face, amazed as always by the brilliant blue of her eyes.

Finally he asked, "What have you heard, Diane?"

"You mean, are they saying you're in trouble?"

"Yes." He smiled faintly. "Right here in River City."

She stopped a forkful of mashed potatoes in midair to consider. "A good crew and a good ship have been lost," she observed. "I think perhaps your friends in the Pentagon E-Ring need a villain."

"Wouldn't you think after years of struggle for an E-Ring office with a window, the brass would settle back and enjoy it? Anyway, as you know, I've been the villain before. It's a familiar role."

"Are you the villain this time?"

"The very worst, in fact. I sink ships and seduce women—the two not necessarily being mutually exclusive, of course."

"You seem to be more successful with the former."

"That's hitting below the belt." He pushed the fruit cup at her. "You eat it; I'm full."

"Harry, was it very bad out there?"

"Have you seen the roster of survivors?"

"Yes."

"The others were my friends too."

"I meant, for you."

"Piece of cake."

"And you really aren't hurt?"

"Just my ego."

"They say that you did it."

"Diane, that's the story of my life. They always say I did it."

"Did you?"

"Truthfully, Diane, I don't know. I wish to God I did know. I told you once that it happened to me before, in the war, and now it's like reliving a nightmare."

"Harry, there's going to be a court of inquiry."

"Oh, I know. There's always an inquiry. Harry St. John's always good for another investigation or two."

"Please don't joke."

"I'm not joking. I'm quite serious, in fact."

"Have you talked to Admiral Cutter yet?"

"No, but I'm going to call him first thing tomorrow."

"He might be able to help you."

"I wish I knew. I don't understand him."

"What do you mean?"

"Well, how does a guy like that get away with saying the kind of things he says about the Navy?"

She looked at him thoughtfully. "Harry, you've been in the service long enough to know that you don't ask that kind of question."

"Mine not to reason why? I think not. It's about time I started asking some questions."

She shook her head sadly. "It seems to me that now's the time you'll have to provide answers. Would you like to tell me about it?"

"No. This conversation is getting much too serious. Please come here now. I was hardly awake when you came in."

She considered the matter gravely and then stepped out of her skirt.

Three

The doctor's name was Jacoby. He probed, thumped, and otherwise tested almost every square inch of Harry's body before finally pronouncing him fit for duty. He confided in Harry his elation at soon quitting the service and going into private practice. With a wink he added that he intended to remain in the Naval Reserve so as to retain his officers-club and post-exchange privileges. There were so many things to buy after eight years of expensive schooling and his relatively slim salary in the Navy. Now he was on the threshold of real money. Then, realizing the difference between the two of them at that moment, he softened his enthusiasm.

"Although sometimes I will envy you guys out there, Commander," Jacoby conceded wistfully as he finished filling out Harry's record card.

"How so, Doc?" It was cold in the examination room, and Harry was glad to slip back into his bathrobe.

"You know what I mean. Booze, women, and cruising the world. Great life in lots of ways."

Harry thought of the tired faces of *Somerset*'s crew, the

deck gang pinched and drawn from the cold Atlantic wind, and the engineers white-faced and grimy from a lifetime spent in a steel cell. If Jacoby had ever gone to sea, he would have found out soon enough that it was a thin existence. "Yeah, it's a great life, all right. Tell that to the crews of *Pueblo, Thresher,* and a few hundred others I could name."

The doctor looked up sharply. "I didn't mean . . ."

"I know what you meant, Lieutenant. Just finish your job."

He was fit—healthier than he had a right to be. Certified ready for duty, he returned to his room to gather up his few belongings. A visitor waited.

"St. John? Jack Hawk's the name. Want to ask you a few questions."

"Sure, why not? You're trial counsel tomorrow, aren't you?"

Hawk nodded pleasantly. "Nothing personal, you know. Have you seen the papers?" He held up a sheaf of clippings, the uppermost of which screamed DESTROYER OFFICER IMPLICATED IN DISASTER. His nails had been professionally manicured, and his hair, cut *en brosse,* was tinted a youthful blond. He stood like a boxer awaiting the bell, squeezing every inch from a short, slight frame. His nonregulation uniform, tailored British Navy fashion—double vents and a watch pocket—advertised success and vanity. This assignment was a plum. Hawk's name was already in the papers.

"I suppose I'm famous?" Harry asked.

"Go ahead, read it."

The essentials of his background were all there, but none of the detail needed to evoke the reality: Irish-American family (eight kids—throw stones at the trains by the house, carefully gather up the coal thrown back at you); former enlisted man (blood, leather, collodion, and a good trainer—Harry, you can be champion of the Atlantic Fleet!); Annapolis (how else do poor boys go to college?); regular

Navy (broken nose, scar tissue on cornea—no glamorous flight or submarine duty); then *Yellowbird* and limbo.

"I reviewed your file and talked to your friend King. You lost a ship before?"

"A minesweep, *Yellowbird,* off Wonsan in the Korean War."

"There was a board of inquiry?"

"I lost one hundred signal numbers for going out of the swept channel to clear my fouled sweeping gear. We hit a mine."

"At least they let you stay in."

"If you can call coding rooms and boat pools fit duty for a career officer."

"And you're one grade behind your classmates?"

Cheaper than severance pay; leave him in till he rots. "Maybe more. I'm still a lieutenant commander; the top of my class is breaking into your grade, Captain."

Hawk studied him carefully: the classic misfit, and yet there was an inner strength there. St. John wouldn't break easily. The trial counsel would have to get at him through his background and his difficulties aboard the destroyer before the collision.

"There are times when I don't like my job, St. John. This isn't going to make the Fleet look good. You're one of us—regular Navy. Your experience with a board of inquiry will help me—at least I don't have to explain the procedure to you. We want to protect the Navy in this, as much as possible."

Harry smiled. "That sounds a little like you might be working up to some sort of a deal."

Hawk shook his head. "No, this isn't Perry Mason. We'll first find out what happened. Right now it looks as though you made a major blunder, ran that destroyer under the carrier's bows, and killed two hundred men. If that is the way it happened, you'll deserve the full penalty and it will be my job to see that you get it."

"Fair enough, Captain. We come out swinging tomorrow. That's at least something I know how to do."

"Again, nothing personal."

They shook on that. Hawk opened the door, but then hesitated. "One last thing, St. John. I understand your assignment to *Somerset* was handled directly by Admiral Cutter, Special Projects, Naval Intelligence. You should know that I called the Admiral. He told me that you were in no way connected with his organization. It's a 'clean case' as far as he's concerned. I'm to proceed on that basis. Do you see it the same way?"

"It's a clean case, Captain. I'll see you tomorrow."

Harry softly closed the door behind Hawk. Clean case? He wished he knew. The Admiral hadn't indicated anything otherwise when they first met.

Some four weeks earlier, the day after Harry had received orders to *Somerset,* he had quite suddenly been relieved of his Washington duties and ordered to a colleague of many years' standing.

To Commander William King, U.S.N., christened "Pozo" by his midshipman contemporaries, Harry's undistinguished career was the embarrassment of their class—a group already graced with several astronauts, one movie star, and a corporate tycoon. The rub was that Ops Twenty had had nothing to do with this assignment; the selection had in fact been made by the Office of Naval Intelligence. And to top that, a vice admiral assigned to the personal staff of the Chief of Naval Operations, none other than the famous Christian "Flank Speed" Cutter, had requested that the briefing about to take place be conducted in the Admiral's own office.

When a vice admiral asks to sit in on a briefing, one does not ask questions. Pozo's curiosity was driving him mad, but he had just time to grab Harry by the elbow and steer him through the long Pentagon corridors to a vast suite that was next to the C.N.O.'s. There, impressed by the blue flag with three white stars upon it and the unfamiliar trappings of very senior rank, the two presented themselves. There was the usual small delay. As the minutes lengthened, Harry found himself diverted by the memorabilia that adorned the walls of the Admiral's outer office. Photographs of kings and presidents beamed down upon them, all autographed with ringing endorsements of the great man inside. The centerpiece of this display was a framed letter to which was attached a small blue-and-white ribbon.

Navy Department
Washington, D.C.

June 30, 1942

CITATION—THE NAVY CROSS

For the display of extraordinary heroism and exceptionally meritorious service while acting as Flag Captain to Commodore, Destroyer Screen, Convoy K-12, when Captain Christian Cutter, USN, did assume command of the flagship during engagement with German battle cruiser *Prinz Eugen.* His vessel heavily damaged, Captain Cutter succeeded in alerting the convoy to the German cruiser's approach. Great loss of life was averted by this timely action.

Out of contact with U.S. forces, all officers including his superior killed, Captain Cutter carried out emergency repairs and navigated his destroyer through enemy waters, arriving eight weeks later with only fifty-three survivors from a complement of one hundred twenty-two.

Then be it known that by the express wish of the Commander in Chief, Captain Christian Cutter, USN, is awarded the Navy Cross in honor of distinguished service, above and beyond the call of duty, and in keeping with the highest traditions of the naval service.

Franklin Knox
Secretary of the Navy

Harry had just finished reading this impressive testimonial when a Seth Thomas marine clock chimed a precise eight bells, and a lieutenant, junior grade, wearing the golden aiguillette of a vice admiral's aide appeared to usher them into the great man's presence.

In addition to his exploits with *Prinz Eugen,* Harry knew that Cutter had earned the nickname "Flank Speed" for pushing his aircraft carriers all over the Pacific at a sustained, boiling thirty-five knots during World War II. Later, he had played a major role in the development of the nuclear carrier, and now, contrary to the official position of the Navy, he was looking a step beyond and urging a cutback in the Navy's budget. Harry had heard the Pentagon rumor that Cutter had been reassigned to a top-secret project for the Navy. Exactly how one managed to publicly differ with the establishment and still enjoy career success was a bit of fancy high stepping that Harry would never understand. It was said of the Admiral that he had strong Congressional support and was the leading candidate of the Armed Services Committees to take over the job of C.N.O. when the present incumbent retired next year.

Chris Cutter rose from behind an almost bare mahogany desk that seemed large enough to serve as the flight deck of one of his famous aircraft carriers.

"Good to meet you, St. John. I find that I have to go up to the Hill unexpectedly, but I did want to see you for only a moment anyway. You may carry on, King."

With a flamboyant wave of his bony hand, the Admiral sank into a soft leather armchair and peeped owlishly at the two of them over a pair of the currently fashionable half-moon spectacles.

Pozo began nervously; he preferred not to have an audience, particularly not a vice admiral, and particularly not *this* vice admiral. "Ah, Harry, in Ops Twenty we like to meet new officers assigned to DesLant and to answer any questions they may have concerning new assignments. In your case, introductions aren't necessary; we've known each other far too long for that sort of business. However, I do want to add my own personal congratulations on your new assignment." He smiled briefly. "A stern chase is a long chase, as they say." Pozo was given to salting his speech with naval maxims left over from his days as a plebe. Harry was by now too hardened to be embarrassed by this clumsy reference to his undistinguished past.

"Thanks, Pozo. What does the operating schedule look like?"

"Not too bad, as I recall. Let's see . . . *Somerset,* wasn't it?" Pozo consulted a slim volume of operating schedules that he had brought with him. "This says that you have plane-guard duty late next week with *Argonne.* Afterward, a short spell of holiday routine in Newport. There's more duty with *Argonne* in, let's see, yes, Operation Iron Strike. Fairly normal schedule for this time of year. You'll have a good chance to break into harness before the fleet exercises next summer."

"Sounds easy enough. When I got my orders, I looked up *Somerset.* She isn't assigned to any particular destroyer division?"

"No, bit of a loner for the moment, I'm afraid. We plan to shift three other tin cans up from Norfolk after Iron Strike." Harry suppressed a smile. He had noticed the Admiral's wince at Pozo's use of the archaic phrase "tin cans" to denote destroyers. Pozo, like other nonseagoing officers, sometimes pushed the "old salt" bit too far. "You'll be all formed up in a proper division, shipshape and Bristol fashion, after Iron Strike."

"What's the Captain like?"

Pozo glanced helplessly at "Flank Speed" Cutter.

"Duke Slattery is a bit unusual, St. John." Cutter had a high-pitched, almost squeaky voice. His long, bony fingers drummed restlessly on the leather armchair. With his thick silver hair laid back along his skull in two symmetrical, bushy turtlebacks, the gaunt features, and his round brown eyes popping out over the tortoiseshell rims of his glasses, he looked more like a schoolmaster than an admiral.

"Slattery came from the merchant marine during the recent officer shortage. Supposed to be a diamond in the rough. You two should get on all right."

Beggars can't be choosers, Harry thought. He asked, "What happened to the former Executive Officer?"

"He was lost at sea." Cutter's voice was expressionless, his manner neutral, as though this sort of thing happened every day.

Pozo broke in. "Now you can see why we need an officer right away. *Somerset* sails this week."

"You mean that I was picked for no other reason than my immediate availability?"

Pozo glanced helplessly at the Admiral. Cutter snorted with impatience. "You were picked for this assignment because you happen to have the exact qualifications we are looking for: lieutenant-commander grade, experience in small vessels, qualified for command at sea, and finally, you are thoroughly grounded in cryptographic work. You will notice that your orders state that, in addition to your duties as Executive Officer, you will be the destroyer's Chief Coding Officer. Unfortunately, *Somerset* currently has no coding officer to assist you. Aside from those qualifications that I have just stated, we need a man as soon as possible. In fact, we need a man aboard *Somerset* right away, certainly not later than this weekend."

Somehow, Harry found himself pleased by that answer. The Navy had not relented; he was just the only man both qualified and available.

"Now that we have disposed of your private little war with the Assignments Branch, St. John," said the Admiral, "supposing that you two go on." He consulted his watch. "I'm due at the House Foreign Affairs Committee in twenty minutes to testify on the military-assistance program." He pulled himself erect from the chair just as his apparently unflappable aide appeared in the doorway bearing the Admiral's cap and braided boat cloak.

"One last thing before I go, St. John. Because the previous Executive Officer took it upon himself to be responsible for coding operations, we are a bit concerned that *Somerset*'s cryptographic activities may not be up to snuff. Ops Twenty has been hellishly long about providing a replacement." He glared at Pozo, who somehow managed a noncommittal expression in the face of this direct criticism. "As one of your first duties, I want you to shake down the code room aboard *Somerset*. I have instructed Lieutenant Halliday at Newport to give you every bit of cooperation. I think you'll find that destruction of some obsolete codes has not been carried out and that *Somerset* has failed to keep up with her full allowance. I would hope that you can get those deficiencies corrected just as soon as possible. When things are straightened out, you can train one of your junior officers to replace you. King, what's the name of that new ensign you sent up to *Somerset* last month?"

"James, I believe, sir. Yes, here he is." Pozo extracted an IBM run of DesLant personnel assignments from his papers. "Ensign Edward James, Admiral. He joined *Somerset* about three weeks ago."

"Good. I thought my memory wasn't failing me. Then, when you are ready, St. John, put Mr. James on the job. Executive officers have more important duties to perform than handling coding chores. Also, if the mess is worse than I fear, get in touch with Lieutenant Halliday right away."

"Yes, sir. Who will transfer the material into my custody, if the former custodian was lost at sea?"

The Admiral blinked. "Why, no one, I'm afraid. I ordered the coding room locked when we received *Somerset*'s signal telling us that Abel was lost. You will make your own inventory against *Somerset*'s allowance and then sign as custodian. All clear?"

"Yes, sir."

"Good. Then I think that does it. I'll leave you in Commander King's hands." He smiled briefly at the two of them. But Harry was still not finished.

"I'm afraid, sir, that I'm still a little confused."

"What don't you understand?" There was more than a hint of quarterdeck authority in the Admiral's voice.

"Well, sir, do I have it all? I mean, I don't believe that it's standard operating procedure for an admiral to personally review the assignment of a destroyer's Executive Officer."

The Admiral's look of exasperation was counterbalanced superbly by the expression of sympathy that crept into King's features.

"Now, look here, St. John, there are many things that you don't know about the Navy, but I'm sure you are aware that the Defense establishment has lately been taking it on the chin from the public. The service wants to be extraordinarily careful. We have a potentially messy situation aboard *Somerset*. I have just explained that the unusual loss of the former Executive Officer has prevented us from making a normal transition aboard your vessel. I want that situation cleared up right away without any nonsense. You are the man who has been assigned that job, and I simply wanted to meet you so that I could tell the Chief that we picked the right man. *I* think we have picked the right man, but if you have any doubts on that score yourself, you should say so at once. Do you have any doubts?"

"No, sir."

The Admiral rose and turned over both palms to signal that the interview was at an end. "Well, then, all I need do further is to wish you smooth sailing, St. John."

They shook hands, and Harry and Pozo departed, the former stifling a wild impulse to bow down and back out.

"Maybe it's just because I'm not used to the altitude in an admiral's office, but I confess that I'm human enough to be impressed. Cutter seems to be all that they say he is." Harry volunteered this assessment as the two officers weaved their way through a large crowd of tourists admiring the portrait of Jim Forrestal that hangs outside the Secretary's office.

Pozo grunted in response. "Turn in here," he said, taking Harry's elbow and steering him around a corner that led to a small snack bar. "You bet he is. He's about the best the Navy's got right now. He's been a White House favorite with both the past and present administrations, even if he didn't have everything else going for him. Here we are!"

The two officers obtained coffee and seated themselves in a quiet booth. The air in the snack bar was stale and permeated with a faint odor of greasy French fries. The coffee was weak and served in paper cups. "Where you're going, you'll have to say goodbye to all of this." With a broad sweep of his hand, Pozo indicated a dozen or so healthy young secretaries in miniskirts who had entered after them. The girls, on their afternoon coffee break, chattered and giggled with irrepressible high spirits as they exchanged tidbits of Pentagon gossip. "Sorry to say, no such lush pastures up in Newport, old boy."

"Pozo, did you ever meet this fellow Slattery?"

"Just once that I can recall. It was during the briefing that we gave him before he took over *Somerset*."

"What do you remember about him?"

Pozo looked embarrassed. "Great big fellow, as I recall. He didn't say much. I can't say that I took to him."

"Is there something else?"

"Well, yes there is, in fact. The fellow that was lost . . . what was his name?"

"The Executive Officer? I don't know."

"Abel, that was it. I remember now. Well, this fellow Abel called us up about a month ago. I seem to remember that he was complaining about Slattery."

"You *seem* to remember?"

"Oh, come off it, Harry. You know what the Operations Center is like. There are almost a hundred ships under our control. You can't remember everything. Besides, you also know what sea duty is like. You get some nut pulled out of a soft shore-duty billet just before he's about to retire, and all he wants to do is run home to the wife and kiddies. Some of these destroyer skippers start playing God, and then everyone aboard gets to his Congressman in a hurry. Happens every week."

"What was Abel complaining about?"

"Hell, I can't even remember. Something to the effect that Slattery had him trapped aboard the ship. Ran him down in front of the crew. That sort of nonsense."

"That was just before Abel was lost overboard?"

Alarm registered in Pozo's chubby features. "Now, just a minute, Buster," he protested. "Don't you go adding two and two and getting five. I have a whole drawerful of complaints from unhappy officers. That doesn't mean that they have to jump over the side."

"No, I guess not. Besides, I guess that I'm getting quite a break."

Pozo nodded wisely. "You bet your sweet ass you are, chum. Frankly, I don't know why you've hung around this long. Most of us would have cleaned up in civilian life." Harry smiled. Pozo had simply stated the regular officer's contempt for the financial capabilities of his contemporaries in the civilian world. Harry knew better. Too many life-insurance salesmen and realtors scratching out a threadbare existence carried calling cards on which their military rank was engraved. And in one bleak moment a few years back, Harry had himself looked outside with an astonishing lack of success.

"But you keep your nose clean on this assignment, Harry, and you'll be right back on the old promotion schedule with the rest of us."

"Sounds easy enough. What's the name of that coding specialist the Admiral mentioned?"

"Uh, Halliday . . . Lieutenant Halliday at Newport Operations."

Four

Clack! The large shade snapped violently as it rolled up, uncovering the diagram. Someone, Pozo presumably, had carefully drawn the paths of the vessels relative to each other up to the moment of collision. Hawk took the wooden pointer, swished it about like a duelist, and stabbed at the crude chalk marks on the blackboard.

"And would you say, Mr. St. John, that this is a fair portrayal of the principal events as they occurred?"

Harry studied the sketch. "Yes," he finally said. "It looks accurate—not to scale, of course."

"Our recorder's artistic talents notwithstanding, let the record show that the witness accepts this diagram as a reasonable facsimile of the principal events."

Hawk was in good form. He tapped the pointer against the soles of his highly polished, expensive shoes and paused thoughtfully as Pozo made the entry. Harry wondered what impression he himself made on the three captains constituting the board: MacDonald, the President, snowy-haired and leathery—a gentle, understanding soul, Harry hoped; Peter Lord, bald, exploding with energy, yet cold, careful; Ed Burnside, an aviator, out of his depth, a man to be easily swayed by Hawk. They stared at him curiously, and Harry sensed he made a sorry appearance, a marked contrast to Hawk's exquisitely tailored elegance. Harry's borrowed uniform was several sizes too small, his white shirt sleeves peeking out of the bunched jacket. He knew he must appear dull, oafish even, in contrast to the polished J.A.G. officer. Hawk was free to roam. Harry was forced to sit rigid, carefully responding to Hawk under oath, every word taken down. Somehow Pozo had managed to get Diane admitted to the proceedings, but Harry couldn't turn around. The witness chair was placed in the center of a semicircle that ran from the recorder, Pozo King, on his left, through the court members to the Marine guard hovering over his right shoulder. Their eyes never wavered from him.

"With the court's indulgence, I'd like now to redirect my questions toward the witness's relationship with his commanding officer, Slattery, who unfortunately did not survive the collision."

MacDonald relit his pipe while he pondered the question. "Is that an issue here, Trial Counsel?"

"Yes, sir. I think it is. Several survivors have offered written opinions that Commander Slattery and Lieutenant Commander St. John were at odds with each other from the day that St. John joined the destroyer. Their apparently frequent arguments may help explain St. John's statement that Slattery was on the bridge at the time of collision. This line of questioning is important because it establishes yet another reason why the witness would choose to demean a brother officer."

Hawk smiled. "Does the phrase 'Red Lead' mean anything to you?" he asked Harry.

"Yes. It was the Captain's nickname for me."

"I see. Would you please explain why he called you that."

Harry squirmed in the chair. It seemed so silly and so long ago.

Sea duty again at last! Like a child on Christmas morning, he had awakened early his first day aboard the destroyer. He glanced about the spartan stateroom of *Somerset* that he had moved into the night before. A long-remembered smell of sea air flooded the small cubicle from an overhead blower, making him feel at home. He rose quickly and had finished dressing when the wardroom steward poked his head through the doorway curtain.

"Name's Willie," the boy introduced himself, taking in St. John and his meager possessions with one fast sweep of wise brown eyes. "Eggs in ten minutes." Without further fanfare, the steward left in search of other officers.

With that cheering news, it took Harry only half the allotted ten minutes to empty his suitcase. Then he briskly mounted the steel ladder alongside his compartment and emerged onto the main deck of the destroyer.

It was a fair but cold day, last night's storm having blown itself out to leave behind frigid, rain-washed air. Two high-flying jets thrummed overhead, lacing long, tapering, torn-cotton contrails across the cloudless sky. Around him, the familiar lean gray ships of the Atlantic Fleet filled the horizon. He strode down the deck, pausing only to read the vessel's nameplate.

USS SOMERSET

Named in honor of Lt. Chauncy Allcott Somerset, a naval hero who distinguished himself during the battle between USS *Chesapeake* and HMS *Shannon* in 1813, USS *Somerset* is the second ship of the fleet to bear the name. Her predecessor, a Union monitor, was sunk during the assault on Mobile Bay, 1863. The present USS *Somerset* was launched at Bath, Maine, in 1944 and was awarded the Presidential Unit Citation for her part in the action off Okinawa, 1945.

The destroyer nested with three other ships far out in the Newport channel. As with other World War II–vintage destroyers, her ribs, spaced exactly thirty-six inches apart, showed plainly through the thin steel of her plating like the bones of an old nag. Her skin, mottled and chromated from bow to stern, carried the honorable scars of hundreds of ungentle dockings. *Somerset,* with steam up and clear decks, was ready for sea. Satisfied with his inspection, Harry made mental note of several "holidays" in the paintwork and then headed below for breakfast. Occasional sailors on deck that morning stared curiously at *Somerset*'s new Executive Officer as he worked his way past them.

The old destroyer's wardroom, with its aroma of bacon and eggs, was cozy and homelike. As he poured himself a mug of coffee, he was joined at table by a rotund, cheerful fellow lieutenant commander.

"You must be St. John, the new Executive Officer. Sorry I missed you last night when you checked in. Name's Charlie Chapman. Officers call me Chappie."

Chappie reminded Harry of Friar Tuck.

"No point in waking you last night, Chappie. The way you were going at it, you sounded like a Burmese sawmill."

"Awful racket, ain't it?" Chapman added. "I can't seem to sleep at sea anymore, so I make up for it in port. Growing old like this pile of old razor blades, I guess." Chapman's cherubic features glowed with a scrubbed, healthy pinkness and an uncomplicated personality. From his service record, Harry knew Chappie was a "mustang"—a former enlisted man, who had risen through the ranks to become the destroyer's Chief Engineer. Harry guessed Chapman was probably good at his job, *Somerset* lucky to have him. They helped themselves to the bacon and eggs on the long platter Willie slid before them.

"Met the Skipper yet?" Chapman's eyes twinkled.

Astonished, Harry replied, "I didn't know he was aboard."

"Oh, yes." Chapman chuckled. "He called for the gig on my watch and came aboard a few hours ago. Decided to sleep it off here, I guess." Chappie's face clouded over. "Look, I understand after you reported aboard last night, you roused the Bosun and took slack out of the moorings. That right?"

"Yeah! She was going up and down like a bronco in that squall last night."

"Well, it's none of my business, but Slattery ain't too happy with what you did. Thought I'd warn you. None of my business, though. He stays out of my engine room, and I give him what he wants." He grinned and added, "If we're lucky, going downsea and downwind, that could even be thirty-four knots."

"What sort of fellow is Slattery?" The blunt question was as much a test of Chapman as of Slattery. Chappie stopped a forkful of steaming bacon in midair.

"There's lots I could say *against* and lots I could say *for* him. He does his job. My worry is the engine room. You'll have to work with him on the bridge. Just make sure you do everything he says. You'll get along."

From outside, they heard a powerful voice raised in anger. The Chief Engineer raised an eyebrow. "If you want to find out what he's like, that sounds like him on the quarterdeck."

Harry rose to his feet. "I guess it's time to present myself."

Twenty feet down the starboard passageway, an enormous bull of a man raged at an obviously terrified young sailor. Harry's immediate impression of Duke Slattery was one of immense strength. *Somerset*'s Commanding Officer must have packed close to two hundred and fifty muscular pounds on a frame that soared well over six feet. Duke Slattery was clothed sloppily in worn black uniform trousers and clumsy fisherman's boots. A black turtleneck sweater stretched to its full limit across an oxlike chest. His massive hands rested heavily on a khaki gunbelt, from which dangled a regulation Colt automatic. The man's narrow-set eyes bespoke a cruel black anger, a kind of evil malevolence that warned the world that Duke Slattery was no one to fool with, at least not in his present mood. As St. John sized him up, Slattery abruptly stopped roaring at the luckless sailor and with one cruel kick to the boy's buttocks painfully assisted his departure.

"Stupid nose-wiper will know better next time," he growled to no one in particular. "No one on my ship violates standing orders, you better believe it!" He pulled off his cap, revealing a skull shaved clean of hair except for a short black band that bisected the top of his head—what sailors call a "white sidewall" trim. Angrily he looked at Harry.

"At last, my new Executive Officer. Here he stands, fresh from Washington, eager for some salt air. All ready to tell me how I want my ship secured."

"Chapman said you probably wouldn't like what I did last night. But I had to take the slack out of the moorings: she was tearing up the fenders."

"So I see, St. John, so I see. Did my overage Chief Engineer bother to tell you the bilge bucket tied to starboard of us had just done her port side in red chromate before that little storm broke yesterday? Come here!"

Pointing down the starboard side, Slattery indicated a broad red smear that now ran the length of *Somerset*'s midship section.

"Now, what would Washington have to say about that, St. John? Or should I call you 'Red Lead'? I had this scow tied up just as you found her because I didn't want *this* to happen. Chapman should have known better than to let you do it—but then, he'll have the next ten days aboard in port to think about it."

St. John fought off a quick, rising sense of outrage. As

eager as Harry was to get off to a good start with his new Commanding Officer, Slattery was making far too much of this. "Chappie shouldn't be blamed, Captain. He didn't know anything about it. In the dark I didn't see the fresh paint."

Slattery regarded him coolly. "Aren't we the proper one, though?" he said sarcastically. "You did a good job of it, at least," he continued with a hint of grudging admiration. "She's tied up tighter than a whore before payday. Okay, Exec, I'll let Chapman off the hook. Come forward, and let's have a drink on it."

The Captain led the way forward to the small cabin that served him when *Somerset* was not at sea. The cubicle was scarcely larger than a good-sized closet and cluttered with worn paperbacks, discarded foul-weather clothes, and out-of-date operational orders that should have been destroyed long ago. Harry noted that not a single photograph or personal memento graced Slattery's desk. The Captain eased himself into a battered chair and pried open the bottom drawer of his desk, in which resposed an almost-empty bottle of cheap whiskey. "Hair of the dog, Red Lead," he explained, tilting his head and letting a good two inches slide down his throat. With a satisfied belch, he pushed the bottle over to Harry, who up until that moment had expected that the invitation to "drink on it" meant coffee. The Captain shrugged his shoulders at Harry's refusal and then settled back and began to read the orders that St. John had given him. Halfway through the single page, a fresh thought suddenly struck Slattery. "Chapman!" he thundered.

The Chief Engineer must have lingered in the vicinity of the wardroom. The word was scarcely out of Slattery's mouth before Chappie stuck his head into the room.

"Give me steam in an hour. We're pulling away from anchorage and heading for the pier to join the ladies and gentlemen."

"Aye, Captain, in an hour. Anything else?"

"Yes. I want two of your snipes for extra duty. Paintwork, starboard side, in case you hadn't noticed. Your watch, you realize."

Chapman ignored the sarcasm. "Aye, Captain. I'll turn over two men to the Officer of the Deck just as soon as the engines are secured." With a sympathetic wink to St. John, Chapman withdrew.

"Okay, Red Lead, this looks genuine enough." Slattery tossed the orders back to Harry. "I guess I'm stuck with you."

"It would so appear," Harry responded dryly. "Is there anything special I should know before I plunge in?"

"Yes. Around here, all my officers get enough rope to hang themselves proper. In general, the bridge and the conning of the ship are my responsibilities, unless I choose to delegate that duty. The engine room belongs to Chapman. You get the paper work." He grinned toothily, revealing small, blackened stumps and a missing incisor. "All disciplinary cases come to me. I expect every officer to put at least three men on report each week. If they don't, they can write themselves up for inattention to duty."

St. John was stunned by this novel disciplinary method. Perhaps this explained the general reputation of *Somerset*. *A strange vessel,* Pozo King had said. *She performs all of her assignments, but from time to time we hear odd things about her. The loss of her Executive Officer, for example. There's nothing you can put your finger on.*

"I suppose the first thing you should do," Slattery continued, "is to inventory all of the confidential material, including the crypto gear we carry in our allowance." Slattery's manner was now a little less unpleasant. "The old Exec wasn't much of a seaman, but he did do that, at least. Things should be in pretty fair shape, you'd better believe it."

"From what I was told, the former Executive Officer was the only man aboard qualified to encode and decode classified traffic."

"That's right, Red Lead. This old dog has been around too long to let some junior ensign get him into trouble. Anyway, we don't get much in the way of classified traffic."

"I see. Then you had better let me have the keys to the crypto shack."

"Keys?" Slattery looked reluctant for an instant. "Oh, yes." He twirled the dial of his small desk safe and, when he had opened the steel door, extracted the bitter end of a halyard, the line cut off three inches below a clamp containing the ship's keys. Pushing back the snap catch, he removed one key and tossed it to St. John, allowing the duplicate to remain on the ring.

"Better let me have both keys—at least until I finish the inventory," St. John suggested dryly.

"Careful bastard, aren't you?" Grudgingly Slattery tossed over the second key.

"Your ship, Skipper. I'm sure you want things letter-perfect. I'll give one of these back to you after I've finished the inventory. Then I'll set about training one of the junior officers to back me up."

"Suit yourself." Apparently Slattery was now bored with the subject. "Better take this Operations Order too." He handed across a thin volume, boldly labeled IRON STRIKE—CONFIDENTIAL, NO FOREIGN DISSEMINATION. "We sail for a few days' work with an aircraft carrier; *Argonne,* I believe it is." His manner now indicated that the interview was over. "Introduce yourself around, Red Lead. I'll see you on the bridge in a few minutes."

Harry found himself more than a little put off by this casual dismissal. Common courtesy called for Slattery himself to at least introduce the ship's department heads to St. John. Furthermore, he reasoned, he was now the second in command of *Somerset.* Surely Slattery had problems other than those in the communications area. If for no other reason than the future efficiency reports Slattery would prepare on St. John, it was important that they establish a good working relationship.

"Perhaps you could outline briefly what you expect of me?"

"Oh, the usual, I suppose. I'll want you to stand some watches under way, since we're shorthanded. You'll be responsible for keeping the ship's office personnel on their toes. You won't have to worry about navigation. Chief Nielson is about as good as you can get, although you will have to keep an eye on him. The wardroom has been running a little slack lately. I'd like you to juice up the junior officers. Get after Ramsey especially, the Gun Boss; he's got girls on his mind all of the time—ass-crazy. Anything I find wrong with the ship, I come to you—you better believe it."

"Sounds like normal Executive Officer duties." Harry volunteered a thin smile.

"Exactly what you wanted from your own Exec on that minesweeper of yours. *Yellowbird,* was it?"

Harry stiffened; so Slattery knew!

"I guess I didn't have my own ship for very long," he responded carefully.

"So I heard, Red Lead. So I heard," Slattery answered. "I'd like to keep this one a bit longer. See you on the bridge."

Chapman met Harry in the wardroom with a sympathetic smile. He studied Harry's face before observing, "He has a way of cutting you down to size, doesn't he?"

Harry shrugged. "Nothing we can't handle, Chappie," he observed optimistically.

"If you can handle Slattery, you'll be the first one that ever did," Chapman replied coolly. Then, remembering the amenities of the situation: "I'd like you to meet Jack Poindexter, our Supply Officer, and Dennis Ramsey, the Gun Boss."

Ensign Poindexter was painfully frail, his sensitive face waxen. Meticulously he dabbed at the corners of his mouth before rising gracefully to offer St. John a soft, girl's hand. He was dressed in crisp new blues with gleaming gold stripes of exquisite French lace. A pungent aroma of sweet-smelling shaving lotion permeated the air about him. Harry smiled.

"First things first. I brought along a copy of my pay record. I'll dig it out and get it to you this morning. Perhaps then you can give me a fill-in on your supply operation."

"Good to have you aboard, sir," Poindexter replied gravely. He smiled uncertainly, his eyes, deep-set and troubled, avoiding Harry's. "Whenever you're ready, there are the usual forms. I'll try and make it painless. Pleased to give you a briefing, too. It's not a complicated operation." His voice trailed off, and he glanced down uncertainly to the Continental breakfast Harry had interrupted. He hates this ship, Harry sensed; most likely terrified of Slattery.

In contrast, Ensign Ramsey pumped his hand vigorously and bellowed a cheerful greeting. Ramsey was a fellow Irishman, a big dark Fenian with sparkling brown eyes and an engaging grin. His collar was torn; his uniform looked as though he had slept in it. Cheerfully he admitted he had been aboard *Somerset* for less than a year—his first assignment, in fact—but already the old destroyer could outshoot anything on the high seas. After Slattery, Harry was glad to learn the wardroom offered at least one person with spirit. Ramsey was delighted to learn St. John was a bachelor.

"Good thing, too, Commander. Skipper poops me out ashore. I like me booze and women, but I can't keep up with him."

The telephone attached to the table buzzed, and Chapman picked up the handset. "Okay," he said after a moment. He looked at Harry. "That was the bridge. You'd better head up there. Looks like we're going in. Slattery likes the sea detail on station early. Lieutenant Tolley asked for you."

Five

"Lord, this is Dandy, read you five by five, out." A thin young officer replaced the radio telephone in its bracket and smiled shyly at St. John.

"Sorry to meet you this way," he apologized. "I'm Tolley, Operations Officer. Let me be the last to welcome you aboard." They shook hands briefly.

"How do things look?" Harry asked.

Before replying, Tolley removed thick glasses and carefully cleaned them with a tissue fished from his foul-weather jacket. He had greenish-blue eyes, the kind that go with red hair and blanched, freckled skin. "All systems are go," he said seriously. "Lines singled up, short stay to the buoy, communications established with Fleet Operations, boilers two and four on the line, and engine-room bells tested."

"Muster report?"

Tolley waved a thumb in the direction of Newport. "Last liberty boat's headed home now."

Outside, a chill north wind scudded the small waves into dull froths that broke occasionally over a whaleboat pounding nestward with the last of the destroyer's weekend libertymen. As cold spray broke over the boat, Harry could imagine the sailors digging deeper into their pea coats trying to ignore the pitching and rolling, the noxious smell of the diesel. Liberty up, an old ship with a tough Skipper, and a brand-new Executive Officer—enough to make a sailor curse. Harry knew what it was like. It was good to have a deck under one's feet again.

"Ensign James reporting for duty, sir."

Harry returned the smart salute. The baby ensign—every ship had one. Even if Harry hadn't already known Ted James was but recently assigned to the destroyer, James's newness was obvious. The other officers had the battered look of men on hard campaign. Ted James, with razor-sharp creases in his trousers, buffed oxfords, and gleaming gold braid, looked as though he had just stepped out of a bandbox.

"Anything you want me to do, Commander?" The question was more a hopeful plea than an inquiry.

Harry took in the pink cheeks and the soft, corn-yellow hair. "I'd be pleased, Mr. James, if you'd keep watch astern from there," Harry said pointing to the Mark 56 gun director. "The Captain will have to rely on your good eyes when he backs out."

"Aye, aye, sir!" James leaped to the ladder with the energy of an uncoiling spring.

The whaleboat had by now been made fast to the gangway, and a chief petty officer checked off the names as the sailors tumbled aboard. A moment later, the phone next to Tolley jangled harshly.

"That was the quarterdeck," Tolley reported. "All hands aboard or otherwise accounted for. Whaleboat will stand clear and follow us in."

St. John picked up the red-painted handset and pushed once, hard, on the button labeled COMMANDING OFFICER.

"Well?"

"St. John here, Captain. Ship's ready in all respects to

get under way." That report was the traditional task of the Executive Officer. It alerted the Captain to the need for his presence on the bridge to take command.

"St. John, do you know where we are supposed to berth?"

"Yes, sir."

"Well, if you need me, I'll be here shaving." Harry heard a soft chuckle, and then the line went dead. Astonished, he felt his throat go suddenly dry. The bastard, Harry thought, he's testing me—almost as though he'd *like* something to go wrong.

"I have the conn," Harry announced, taking small comfort in Tolley's expression of sudden confusion. "Quartermaster, enter in the log, 'Executive Officer has the conn with Lieutenant Tolley as Junior Officer of the Deck." Slattery could have waited, given him a chance to feel his way with the ship. Extracting her from the center of a destroyer nest was like being thrown to the wolves. "Mr. Tolley, pass the word: 'Take in all lines—stand by to get under way.' "

"Then the name 'Red Lead' was in fact a reminder of your first blunder aboard the destroyer?" Hawk rolled a piece of chalk back and forth in his open palms. The chalk made loud clicking noises as it rolled against his Annapolis ring.

"I guess you could say that. The nickname didn't bother me."

"Didn't it?" *Click-click!* "We shall see. Did not Slattery then ask you to take the destroyer to the pier? Did you not then make another mistake?" *Click-Click!*

"The damage to *Pickering* was minor. The ship's davits weren't secured. When we backed out of the nest, the wash made *Pickering* roll. The whaleboat swung outboard. We couldn't stop, of course."

Hawk's eyes widened. "A motor whaleboat lost, and you call that minor? I don't call it minor, especially when Commander Slattery had a spotless record of good seamanship.

The duty officer at Newport Operations didn't think it so minor. *He* reported it to Washington."

Pozo King stopped his pencil in midair. He remembered *that* message. He remembered because someone else had thought it important.

The night after *Somerset* crushed *Pickering*'s whaleboat, Pozo had been fetched from a television special depicting the murky, brutal history of the National Football League in order to answer a call from Operations Center.

The duty officer, a conscientious WAVE ensign, had reported simply that a message had just been received alerting Ops Twenty to modest damage that had occurred to a destroyer at Newport. The WAVE was puzzled because the message had originated at Newport Operations, rather than from one of the involved vessels, as would have been the normal procedure. Pozo's first impulse was to ignore the matter completely. He often received such nonsense in the evening, and part of his job, in fact, was to decide between wheat and chaff and pass the wheat upward. Then, on sudden inspiration, he asked, "Was *Somerset* one of the vessels involved?"

"Why . . . yes, sir!" Surprise at his clairvoyance edged into the WAVE's voice.

"Does the message mention the responsible officer by name?"

"Yes, sir . . . a Lieutenant Commander St. John, it says."

"Hold on to that message, baby. I'm coming right over."

Tooling down the Columbia Pike in his ancient Rambler, Pozo found himself amused at this small *accident* involving his classmate. It was hard enough to keep the black-shoe Navy running these days without having to put up with the kind of political influence from Cutter's office that had swung St. John's appointment. Pozo himself had considered taking the *Somerset* Executive Officer billet, but he had finally decided that the assignment would be too humiliating for him, since many of his classmates were already getting their own commands. However, to have that upstart, that class disgrace, Harry St. John, forced upon him was something else again. It was uncharitable, he knew, but he couldn't help relishing the consternation Harry must have felt at this small mishap afloat, just when he would be trying so hard to make good. There was poetic justice in real life after all.

The WAVE was a saucy little thing with big brown eyes and a skirt that was so tight that the design of her girdle showed through clearly. This was her first night duty, and she was obviously pleased that she had guessed right and picked the one message in a hundred that would bring the Commander from his home. As she leaned across the desk to get the telegram, her blouse fell open, revealing a white lace bra. Pozo had to fight hard to resist the impulse to suddenly plunge his hand into the opening. He marked the girl for future attention. Under Pozo's management, a co-operative WAVE could go far, especially when the wife and kids were out of town.

The message was not as damning as he had hoped. In fact, the damage reported was apparently so slight that he wondered why he had been notified. Then he put two and two together and came up with Vice Admiral Cutter. The chance to spoil the old man's evening by revealing his protégé's boner, at the same time scoring a point for Ops Twenty, was irresistible.

But the Admiral wasn't at home, and it was only on second thought that Pozo decided to try his office. The clock read after ten in the evening by this time, but surprisingly, Cutter's irritating whine came over the wire.

"King here, Admiral. Sorry to disturb you, but . . ."

"Yes, yes?" came the testy response.

"I wanted to call your attention to a message that just came in from Newport Operations. It concerns *Somerset.*"

"Indicator oh-two-oh-one-two-five Zulu?"

"Why, yes," Pozo admitted with surprise.

"I received it at eighteen thirty-four local time, young man. Anything else?"

"Ah, no, sir," replied Pozo, completely taken aback.

"Well, then . . ." The telephone buzzed as the line went dead.

"And what was Slattery's reaction to this 'minor' damage to *Pickering*?"

"He . . . ah . . . confined me to the ship for a week."

"I see," said Hawk dryly. Musing aloud, he drove home his point. "Unusual . . . second in command . . . punished before the crew for lubberly ship handling."

MacDonald glanced at his watch and cleared his throat. "I think we should stop here, gentlemen, and reconvene tomorrow. Are you finished with this witness, Trial Counsel?"

"Yes, sir. Tomorrow I'd like to summon Lieutenant Jacoby, the doctor who examined the witness. There is a question as to his physical state the night of collision. I'm finished for the moment, sir."

"Let's adjourn, then." MacDonald smiled. "I'd like to catch them at the Pentagon before they go home."

However, one of those on Captain MacDonald's calling list could not be reached. Admiral Cutter had received a late-afternoon visitor and left instructions not to be interrupted.

"You say you are with O.N.I., Lieutenant Hunter?"

"Yes, sir." Henry Hunter was short and stocky. He wore civilian clothes—one of the new knit suits and a wide, salmon-colored tie that Cutter found particularly obscene. "We made a routine check on the *Somerset* business, and turned up something out of the ordinary. I thought I'd best report it to you."

"That was?"

"Before the destroyer left Newport, there was an unusually large payroll withdrawal from Navy Disbursing. Further, the Commanding Officer cashed a large check against his personal account. The check was made out to the Foundation for Non-Theatrical International Events."

"Why I'm an honorary trustee of that institution!"

"Yes, sir. An odd coincidence."

"But how does all this concern me?"

Hunter smiled. "It doesn't, as far as we know, sir. However, your office has been working on the Truxton Cipher's leak . . ."

"You know about that?" the Admiral interrupted sharply.

"Yes, sir . . . and I was given to understand *Somerset* was one possible source you had under surveillance."

Admiral Cutter made a tepee of his palms and considered the matter thoughtfully. "Hunter, I'm afraid the *Somerset* file is closed now. We never turned up anything irregular on that particular ship—certainly nothing that might even suggest a compromise of the Truxton Ciphers system." The Admiral glanced at his watch. He looked outside to the now-deserted parking lot.

"Yes, sir. Except the money . . ." Hunter pursued.

"Nonsense," snorted the Admiral. "I know the Foundation. Worthwhile organization—in fact, affiliated with the U.N.; that's why I let them use my name. And if the ship's Supply Officer chose to keep a large amount of cash on hand, that's not unusual either."

"I guess not, sir." Henry Hunter rose to leave. "You are continuing the Truxton Ciphers investigation?"

"Of course. My instructions are to trace down the leak. The collision simply eliminates *Somerset* as a source to be further investigated." He sighed "Unhappily, that still leaves a large number of other possibilities."

His hand on the doorknob, Hunter paused. "By the way, what do you think will happen to that fellow St. John up at Newport?"

The Admiral's eyes narrowed. "Most of my career has

been spent at sea. I'm proud of my profession. St. John had his chance with that minesweeper. Now the destroyer—two hundred men went down with her. If I had it in my power, I'd put him away for life."

News of the court of investigation within the Naval War College spread. Outside, young students, idlers, and activists bent on embarrassing the defense establishment had gathered to exploit the occasion. Harry's departure from the weathered old fortress set off a great noisy clamor, surprising for the intensity of its hatred. Until freed by a score of Marines, he was momentarily the mute victim of a galaxy of exploding flashbulbs, jeers, and a tangle of microphones that swam before him like cobras.

Aware of the crowd's potential for violence, the Commanding Officer of the naval base had assigned an enormous Negro steward to patrol the corridor outside Harry's room in the B.O.Q. It was clear from the manner in which the steward laid a two-foot nightstick into his palm that he was untroubled by any moral issues involved in the employment of his oaken mace. "Don't you fret, Commanda. Nobody gets by Amos." Should the Navy decide to restrict his movements, Harry realized that Amos, of course, would quietly serve another purpose.

Alone in his room, Harry discovered a parcel sent over from *Argonne*. Packed neatly inside were the salt-stained clothes he had worn on the night of collision. Harry shook out the clothes and hung them up in the closet. In the process, he discovered a thick, square object crammed into his back trouser pocket. Puzzled, he drew it forth. It was Slattery's Night Order Book—water-swollen and bent, but still legible. He tossed it on the desk and began to thumb through it idly as he dialed Diane. There was no answer from her room. He always had trouble getting her on the phone—beginning with the night they first met.

Six

His first day on the destroyer was already a day to remember and it wasn't even over yet. One thing after another had gone wrong. Finally, in desperation, he had had to disobey Slattery's order confining him to the destroyer. As the nightly officers' movie rumbled on in the wardroom, he had climbed ashore over the propeller guards, dug out his snow-covered car, and driven to the officers' club. There, a well-earned Scotch and soda warming his insides, he found HALLIDAY, D., LT. in the naval-base directory. He argued his way past an officious petty officer who complained the B.O.Q. switchboard was normally closed after ten thirty P.M. Finally he made the connection.

"Hello?" The woman's voice (apparently some things were permissible in the B.O.Q. after twenty-two thirty) was sleepy, her manner irritable.

"May I speak to Lieutenant Halliday, please?"

"Who?"

"Lieutenant Halliday of Newport Fleet Operations."

"This is she."

He cursed his luck. Halliday was a WAVE—probably

battleship-sized, virginal, and at the moment wearing wrapper and hair rollers. He plunged ahead anyway.

"Name's St. John—Lieutenant Commander." Rapidly he sketched in the events leading to his transfer. By the time he got to the purpose of his call, she interrupted angrily.

"Look, Commander, if this is some cheap way to get a date . . ."

Women, he thought. The Colonel's lady and Judy O'Grady.

"Calm down, sister," he pleaded. "I was told to get in touch with you by Admiral Cutter if I found anything missing from *Somerset*'s cryptographic allowance. I have, and so I'm getting in touch with you."

"Admiral who?"

"Cutter. Vice Admiral Cutter."

"Oh, yes. Now I recall seeing something on you. It's almost eleven; can't we do this in the morning?"

"I'm afraid I'll have some problem getting ashore the next few days. I'd prefer to get this over with now."

"Well, we certainly can't meet here," she snapped.

He stifled a sarcastic reply.

"Where are you now?"

"Officers' club, down the hill from the War College."

"Give me twenty minutes."

He ordered another Scotch and waited her out. He had plenty to think about.

After a cheerless supper with the duty section, he had made his way to Radio Central and unlocked the coding room. Expecting the customary paranoid neatness of shore-station cryptographic centers, he shook his head in wonderment at the scene before him.

Spools of unwound message tape festooned the area like the morning after a New Year's Eve party. Rotting fruit cores, green moldering banana peels, cigarette ends, and discarded paperbacks littered the area. In one corner of the small room, a tower of uncorrected Hydrographic Office publications had toppled, cascading classified folios across the rusting steel deck. Even the room's one small chair rested haphazardously on three legs. That wasn't all, however.

What most astonished Harry was the mural that swam before his unbelieving eyes. It was as though someone had attempted to depict the entire erotic range of the Kama Sutra—a pornographer with only crude artistic talents but the ambition of a Michelangelo. Male and female sexual anatomy had been portrayed in every conceivable circumstance. When the author's instinct for straight pornography had begun to fail him, he had finished up his work with a crudely done tableau of religious scenes incorporating his earlier offerings. It had taken Harry the better part of an hour to scrub the walls clean and remove the litter. During the course of his cleanup, he concluded that the officer he had replaced, Lieutenant Commander Abel, must have been either insane or driven that way aboard the destroyer.

And there was yet another problem, one that wouldn't wash away. Harry had carefully inventoried the equipment carried on the destroyer's allowance list. Three coding devices in the Truxton Cipher series were missing. Had Slattery known this when he restricted Harry to the ship? The loss of the equipment had to be reported to Fleet Operations right away. It would make Slattery look bad, but the hell with it. He had his own instructions from Admiral Cutter.

Cutter must have suspected *Somerset* was a fouled-up nightmare. That was why he had assigned Harry in the first place. "Potentially messy situation," the old Admiral had said. "Get it straightened out—paper work, everything." Had he had any idea of what he asked?

The Ship's Office was administered by Elsworth, a plump, prissy yeoman. His name and mincing manner had inspired the crew to tag him "Elsie." Unhappily, Harry had to admit the nickname was appropriate. That afternoon Elsie had poured out a torrent of complaints in an annoying, nasal whine. He was not getting any cooperation from the engineers: "Those dirty men are simply outrageous, Commander"; personnel were transferred without notification to the Ship's Office; the Captain passed around liberty cards on whim. "I don't even have an accurate Watch Bill," Elsie finally admitted.

"Then how in hell do the men know they have a watch?"

"The chiefs and senior petty officers assign them as they feel like it."

Oh, ho! Harry thought. I've seen that before. Control the crew by using the Watch Bill for punishment.

"Okay, Elsworth. Put a notice in the Plan of the Day giving the division officers twenty-four hours to turn in a permanent Watch Bill. Any changes from then on will require my personal approval."

"Please, sir," Elsie whined, "we don't even put out a Plan of the Day."

"What?" Harry exploded. He rolled up his sleeves. "Elsworth, stand by to go to press. I'll write this first one, and from now on you'll turn one out every day."

But it was going to be an uphill battle. He was paying for Abel's incompetence.

Harry finished his Scotch and looked up to signal the waiter. Framed in the doorway, a young WAVE officer was staring at him uncertainly. She was an agreeable surprise! More than good-looking, Lieutenant Halliday was strikingly attractive. She was also obviously irritated at having to keep this unscheduled appointment. Her blue eyes explored the room restlessly as she tip-tapped a slender foot and waited for Harry to make himself known. Now he understood her suspicions as to the nature of his call. He rescued her from the stag line at the bar just in time.

"Halliday? I'm Harry St. John. Thanks for coming."

"You didn't tell me about the snow."

"If I had, you wouldn't have come."

She slid into the booth, and the stag line did a disappointed about-face. He ordered a Drambuie for her before briefly describing the mess he had discovered in the destroyer's Crypto Center and revealing the loss of the Truxton Ciphers. When he had concluded, she regarded him with a puzzled expression. She asked, "Well, what do you do now?"

"I was hoping you could give me the answer to that question. This *is* O.N.I. business, isn't it?"

"Yes and no," she replied evenly. "I'll make the report to Washington, if that's what's worrying you." She took from him the card on which he had noted the serial numbers of the missing equipment. "Yes, it checks," she said. "This equipment was all recently issued."

"You'll report this to Admiral Cutter?"

"Perhaps."

Smart little girl; she wasn't telling him anything she didn't have to. "Your job's finished, Commander. You won't get into any trouble." He could have wished for more sympathy in her tone.

"I'm the nervous type when classified material is missing."

The snowflakes frosting her hair had now turned to shining droplets. Her face was quite pink in the warm room. "Don't be nervous—unless, of course, *you* took the rotors."

He laughed. "Not a chance, baby. What were Cutter's instructions to you?"

She measured him coolly before replying. "To treat you like anyone else, but with one exception. Normally if we found classified material missing, we would report it directly to Naval Security. In this case, Cutter asked that we report to him instead. He has that authority if he chooses to use it."

"In other words, Cutter expected this?"

"That I couldn't say. I might know more after I talk to Washington tomorrow."

"Who is he, anyway?"

"What you really mean is, just what does his particular project have to do with you? The answer is, nothing as far as I know, and that's all I'm going to tell you." She glanced at her watch. "Look, I'd better be going."

"You mean that he's working on something really big?" He found himself wondering what she would look like in a bikini. Probably all bones and angles.

"Not at all, Commander. I don't know what he's working on, nor do I care. As far as you and I are concerned, this is strictly routine business."

"Was the other Executive Officer mixed up in this?"

"I don't know."

"But you knew him?"

"No. That is, I only heard about him."

"Did you know his name?"

"Abel, I believe."

"One last question: how do I know that this fellow Cutter is on the up and up?"

"You'll just have to take my word for it, Commander," she replied with more than a hint of sarcasm. "You can trust him. After all, he is a vice admiral."

"Why don't you try calling me Harry?"

"There's nothing more that I can tell you. Now I must leave."

"When will I see you again?"

"The next time you stop by Newport Operations, I suppose. When the restriction to your ship is lifted, that is."

"We sail on Thursday, but that's only for two days. We'll be back in on Saturday morning. Perhaps we could arrange to have dinner on Sunday night. I mean, Cutter *might* have some instructions for me after you report this to him. What's the name of that lobster place—Nick's?"

"No, I'll probably have to go to Washington this weekend." Seeing the disappointment in his face, she relented. "It's a regular thing, nothing to do with you. I usually fly back on Monday morning, but I suppose I could just as easily make it on Sunday night if we ate a little late."

"Anytime you say."

"Make it nine, then. And if you don't mind, I'd prefer Gunder's. It's over at Tiverton, and the lobster is a better buy for the money." This observation seemed to fit her so well that it made him smile.

"What's so funny?"

"Nothing. Let's leave it at that. I'll be at the B.O.Q. at eight-thirty or so this Sunday night."

"You'd better call first. I'll most likely be back by then, but I wouldn't want you to make the trip for nothing. I'll leave word at the desk."

"I'll take my chances." He wanted a full commitment on her part. "Now may I give you a lift back?"

"My car is just outside. Finish your drink."

"Hey!" he said as she rose. "I don't even know your first name."

"Diane," she replied evenly.

Good and bad sides to everything, he thought after she had left. I finally get back to sea, but my ship turns out to have a screwball Skipper. Now I'm caught up in some stupid O.N.I. investigation of the sloppy handling of classified material—but that leads to the cool but damned attractive Miss Halliday.

Well, things were looking up. At least he was back in the mainstream, and that was a sight better than steering a desk in Washington. Now, if only he could get back aboard *Somerset* unobserved.

Seven

Jacoby lolled in the witness chair, flaunting his soon-to-be-civilian status like a red flag.

"Dr. Jacoby, I believe you conducted a complete medical examination of St. John when he arrived at the hospital?"

"No, sir. I gave him a fast checkup and a sedative. The following morning I gave him the full examination."

Hawk looked annoyed. "Is that standard procedure?"

"Of course it is. If you wanted him examined on arrival, why didn't you say so? How many doctors do you think we have over there?"

"But you did perform the complete examination the next day?"

"I already said I did."

"In *that* examination, then, did you find alcohol in his blood—any evidence that St. John might have been intoxicated on the night of collision?"

"Of course not."

"I see. Now, Dr. Jacoby, I don't pretend to know anything of the physiological effects of liquor, but it's my understanding alcohol is absorbed and rather quickly burned off. That correct?"

"Depends. The average highball can be accommodated into the system in about an hour. Several factors involved —alcoholic concentration, food in the stomach, speed of drinking. Read the research paper done by the Karolinska Institute in Stockholm. When did the collision occur?"

"Just before midnight."

"That would leave an elapsed time of forty hours. Then, medically speaking, there is no way of knowing."

"If I may summarize what you are saying, Doctor . . ." Hawk leaned forward and stressed the words. "You cannot say whether or not St. John was drunk, or otherwise unfit for duty, the night of collision. That correct?"

"Yes."

"Then by the same token, St. John *could* have been intoxicated when the collision took place?"

Jacoby shrugged his shoulders. "He could have been bombed out of his skull and I wouldn't have known it."

Hawk smiled. "That's all, Doctor. Chief Nielson, please!"

Lars Nielson's light blue eyes shifted uneasily, his bandaged hands protectively held in his lap, as he took the chair vacated by Jacoby. Nielson was an excellent quartermaster, a first-rate navigator like his ancestors who had long ago sailed their longboats through fog-shrouded fiords. However, the court of inquiry was a new experience, and he was nervous.

"The night of collision, when did you arrive on the bridge, Chief?"

"Just a few moments before collision, sir."

"And did you see Commander Slattery at that time?"

"No, sir."

Hawk glanced meaningfully at the three members of the court. "In your statement you said you thought Mr. St. John had been drinking the night of collision."

"Yes, sir."

"That's a very serious allegation. Did you actually see him take a drink that night?"

"No, sir. But he had been drinking all the same."

"How did you know?"

Nielson smiled. "Hell, I got too many years in this man's outfit not to know *that.* He was reeling around on the bridge, he had just puked, and you could smell the booze. What more do you want?"

"My God," Peter Lord exploded, as a loud murmur swept the room. MacDonald pounded his fist for silence. Hawk, looking pleased with himself, picked up a piece of chalk. When order had been restored he asked, "Chief, in your opinion, did St. John and Slattery get on well together?"

Nielson glanced at Harry before replying. "I wouldn't say so, sir."

"Oh!" *Click click!* "What seemed to be the trouble?"

"Well, sir, take the Ship's Office. We chiefs and petty officers used to do a pretty good job of running the ship. Then along came St. John and he changed everything. He allowed the yeoman that ran the Ship's Office to override the chiefs. And right from the start he seemed to have it in for anyone the Captain liked."

"Anyone in particular?"

"Well, Dieter, the Captain's Coxswain, for instance."

Harry whistled as he read the message. He had slipped ashore the preceding night for nothing. All old Truxton Cipher rotors were discontinued, and DesLant would issue a complete replacement set to all ships that morning. But since last night, *Somerset* had been moved to a Mike buoy to load ammunition. Still, orders were orders; Slattery would have to let him go.

"The trip shouldn't take long, Captain. But you'll have to lift my restriction to the ship for an hour or so."

"One hour *if* the gig doesn't break down, and *if* you can

find the fleet landing in this pea soup." Slattery indicated the fog that swirled about them with a wave of his hand. "We have to *share* my gig with *Pickering* these days," Slattery complained. "Well, go ahead, if you must. Chappie, see if you can give us an engineer that will make that Swiss watch run for a change."

"I'll start her up myself," the Chief Engineer volunteered.

If anything, the fog seemed to have thickened by the time the two officers had assembled a boat crew and Chappie had coaxed the small diesel into complaining life. With the boat's engine idling uncertainly, Harry fretted over the course they should take to find the fleet landing through the fog.

"If I was doing it, St. John, I'd head east until I hit the beach," Chapman yelled as he fiddled with the fuel intake to the small engine. Each chug of the diesel seemed more confident under his talented fingers.

"What's wrong with the engine?"

"Nothing really. The damned thing is always breaking down because Dieter here likes to think of himself as the Barney Oldfield of the waves." As Chappie climbed out of the boat, he stabbed a thumb in the direction of the boat's Coxswain—a chunky, middle-aged sailor who scowled unpleasantly at the two officers.

"Keep her headed zero-nine-five, Dieter, once we clear the fantail," Harry said. The sailor simply grunted in acknowledgement.

The diesel roared briefly, and with a musical bubble about the stem, the little boat made off quickly. Moments later, *Somerset* disappeared as though into a cloud. The fog hung thickly about them, deadening sound and limiting visibility to less than a few yards. Small droplets of water condensed on the canvas canopy as they sped through the moisture-laden air. At length, Harry heard the boom of a foghorn from what seemed miles away. "Slow down,

Dieter," he said. Apparently deafened by the roar of the engine, the Coxswain ignored him. Harry climbed over a thwart and partially closed the throttle, the boat immediately pitching forward as it fell off the step. This time the mournful blast of the foghorn seemed much nearer. Harry glanced at the small boat compass. The heading read thirty degrees to the right of course. If they stayed on it, they would pass Newport and go right out to sea. Harry glared at the Coxswain.

"I'll take the tiller, Dieter."

"Captain don't let anybody handle the gig but me." Dieter, regarding him coolly, made no move to yield the helm.

"I said I'd take the tiller, Dieter. Don't make me say it again!" Still the sailor clung stubbornly to the oakum-wrapped rod, his expression defiant. Finally his glance wavered and fell away. With a shrug of the shoulders he abandoned the helm and crawled forward under the canopy. Harry retrieved the flailing tiller and brought the boat around in a wide arc. They were far off the course Harry had intended, and he could now only guess at a heading that would take them to the boat landing. Moments later the fog thinned, and he spotted the green copper roof of the War College, then groped his way forward into the channel.

Diane seemed surprised to see him. He tossed the empty sack on the counter by way of explanation. "Last night you must have known the code was to be changed. Couldn't you have told me?"

"Even if I'd known, I couldn't tell you."

"Wouldn't have is more like it."

She shrugged her shoulders. "How did you get here? I thought we just moved you out to Mike Twelve."

He smiled. "It's nice to know someone's always watching over you."

A young flag lieutenant with a dazzling smile and elegant new uniform of soft, extravagant cashmere interrupted them. "Staff conference in twenty minutes, Diane," he reminded the girl.

"Thanks, Bill. I'll be along shortly."

"And we *are* having lunch today with the Commodore?"

"If he's still serving that fabulous *blanc de blancs,* how could I refuse?"

Harry, acutely aware of his own dirty foul-weather clothes and the morning stubble he had been too busy to scrape from his embarrassingly prominent chin, noticed the Flag Lieutenant had extraordinarily long, soft-appearing eyelashes. One set dipped in Harry's direction.

"I'll see that a bottle is put on ice right away. Don't be late, now." With that reminder, he hurried away.

"And *I* was going to buy you *coffee,*" Harry said.

"Not a chance. It looks like it'll be a long morning here with the rotor changes to make."

"Maybe, then, you better get on with your busy morning and your fabulous *blanc de blancs* with the Commodore."

She smiled slowly. "Don't misunderstand. It's just that one gets a little used to the fast pass around here. Just reflexes, that's all."

His turn to smile.

"And if you are interested," she continued, "it's rumored around here that the Flag Lieutenant doesn't care for girls."

He laughed at that. "I hope someone warned the Commodore."

"The Commodore can take care of himself. I suspect you can too."

"Why me?"

"Well, I heard you were shaking things up on your ship—Plan of the Day, watch bills, that sort of thing."

"Who told you that?"

"I have an admirer aboard *Somerset*."

"Two admirers. Who's the other one?"

"Your young ensign, Ted James. We had him here for two weeks while your ship was at sea."

Harry chuckled. "In the future, I'll see he has better things to do than chase after good-looking WAVES."

"Don't you dare. He's cute. Besides, how else can I check up on you?"

"If that's the relationship, I don't mind at all."

She filled his sack, carefully listing the serial numbers of the new rotors before placing them in the bag. When all was ready, she sealed the canvas top with drawstring and lead slug. "Here's your receipt," she said. "Now I really had better go. It's considered bad form to keep the Commodore waiting at staff meeting."

"And Sunday night?"

"I'll try, Harry."

That at least put a new complexion on a morning begun so wretchedly, Harry thought, walking down the hill. But when he reached the gig and swung aboard the heavy bag of new coding equipment, he was annoyed to discover the boat crew short one man.

"Where's Dieter?" he asked the engineer.

The sailor put down a tattered comic book. "Dunno, Commander. He said something about going to the P.X."

"When was that?"

"About thirty minutes ago."

Directly off the landing a gleaming admiral's barge had appeared, her crew at parade rest, her powerful engines thundering with short bursts of power to maintain position. Harry was aware *Somerset*'s greasy launch stood out clearly among the craft filling the pier. He was also aware of the loading and unloading going on from the other launches. Only *Somerset*'s gig crew lounged indolently as their boat wallowed in her own oil slick. The admiral's barge carried a blue flag with two white stars. As Harry watched, a flash of gold appeared in the stern cabin. That settled it.

"Bear a hand on those lines," Harry said. "We're going home." The engineer carefully folded up his comic book before replying. "Dieter ain't back yet. Who's going to take the tiller?"

"I am."

"Dieter ain't going to like this."

"He'll like it even less when he gets back and finds he's on report. Now start that engine."

It was a long, cold ride back to *Somerset,* Harry's mood not improved by the drenching he received as the little boat clawed upwind. They tied up at the low stern, where Harry could easily climb up to the fantail. He changed from his wet clothes and carefully stored the new crypto system in the coding room. Elsworth was hard at work in the Ship's Office by the time Harry finally got there.

"Know how to make out a charge slip for inattention to duty?"

"Sure," Elsworth replied. "Who's the culprit and what were the circumstances?"

"Dieter took it upon himself to visit the P.X. without permission. We had to leave without him."

The yeoman neatly tore apart the blank charge slip. "If you said Dieter, Commander, I'll save you the trouble."

"What do you mean by that?"

"Dieter must have been written up a hundred times. Not once has the Captain ever found him guilty."

"I don't understand."

"Commander, I'm trying to tell you Dieter's the Captain's favorite. As long as the gig runs, Mr. Slattery lets him get away with murder. You'll never make a charge against him stick." The yeoman giggled as he related this latest piece of *Somerset* scandal.

"Not anymore, Elsworth. You write him up. I'll see it sticks."

"I wouldn't bet on it, Commander. But I sure want to be around when it happens."

Eight

Hawk paced slowly back and forth, his shuffling palms thoughtfully raised in a gesture of prayer. "I believe you said, Lieutenant Tolley, the relationship between St. John and Slattery was not the best."

"That's right, sir."

"And how did you come by that opinion?"

Paul Tolley looked momentarily embarrassed. "Why, everyone on the ship knew that!"

"Yes, but what led *you* to that opinion?"

"Well, they were always arguing . . ."

"For example?"

Tolley's annoyance showed. He was being asked to explain the obvious. "Okay," he finally said. "Everyone knew Commander Slattery didn't like what St. John was up to. Once during a gunnery exercise, St. John kept protesting the Captain's orders . . ."

That morning *Somerset* and *Pickering* had been dispatched to carry out antiaircraft exercises with an old Skyraider from Quonset Point. The two destroyers, in line astern, awaited the arrival of plane and target. *Somerset* was at Battle Stations, her five-inch guns loaded with live rounds. The two ships had slowed until they barely wallowed in the sluggish seas. Dennis Ramsey, his features half hidden beneath an enormous helmet that flared to accommodate special communications gear, perched on the Mark 56 director and awaited the Captain's orders. But Slattery, other than glancing aft at the swirling upheaval that marked their progress and warning the helmsman to "get those assholes out of the wake," fell into a brooding silence. Harry let his mind wander back to a discussion with Elsworth an hour before.

"The chiefs are furious, Mr. St. John," the chubby yeoman had confided. "I mean, now that we are running things from the Ship's Office." Elsie, backed by the authority of the Executive Officer, was a new man. In a twinkling the mess that was the official records center had disappeared, largely thanks to unrequested overtime put in by the yeoman. The small office had been scrubbed out and repainted. Harry hesitated to use the ashtrays, which the fussy Elsworth emptied before Harry had finished smoking.

"What makes you say that, Elsworth?"

"Well, I heard that Chief Nielson went to see Mr. Slattery about it."

"And what did the Duke say?"

"I understand he was furious, but he sent for Navy Regulations and found you were right. Didn't he say anything to you about it?"

Harry was both exasperated and amused. Elsworth's probing resembled a protective woman's concern over the business affairs of her husband. "No, he didn't, Elsworth. And you can't argue with Navy Regs!"

"*That* never bothered Slattery before."

Suddenly Slattery's telephone talker snapped alert and pressed the phones tight against his ears. "Lookout reports plane in sight, starboard quarter, Captain." Harry paralleled his binoculars with those of the lookout and scanned the northern sky. A wisp of smoke from *Somerset*'s after stack obscured his view for a moment; then the yellow-brown fog thinned and he spotted the plane. Kiting along at a bare hundred knots, the Skyraider had just finished streaming the target and was lining up for the initial starboard-side run.

"Baker at the dip," thundered Slattery. With a great squeal, a tattered red flag rose from the signal bag and came to a stop halfway up to the yardarm. Harry switched on the ship's loudspeaker system.

"Now hear this," he said, the words roaring about him from the bridge speaker. "*Pickering* will fire first to starboard. This will be a nonfiring—repeat, nonfiring—run for us."

As Harry stepped back outside, *Pickering* opened up with her main battery. Yellow flame sprang from her gun muzzles, and black, debris-laden smoke erupted outboard along her starboard side. After a short interval, small black tufts of smoke appeared in line alongside the path of the target, followed by the sound of bursting shells.

"Look at her, look at her!" thundered Slattery. "That's damned good shooting. She's getting a burst with every round. Right on target."

Harry squinted over the bridge pelorus. "Target approaching bearing, Captain. Stand by. . . . Mark bearing!"

"Commence, commence, commence!" yelled Slattery.

Ah-Ooga, Ah-Ooga, sounded the klaxon alarm. *Somerset*'s mute cannon tracked the target until plane and tow were full on the bow. "Mark bearing, Captain," Harry said as plane and tow passed out of the firing sector.

"Cease firing, cease firing, cease firing," Slattery ordered. The klaxon sounded again. Baker was hauled down from the yardarm. The practice run was over.

"Don't be in such a bloody hurry on the firing run, Red

Lead. The more shells we put in the air, the more likely we are to get bursts."

"Captain," Harry protested, "the Operations Plan defines the firing sector as the ninety degrees between broad on the bow and broad on the quarter. Anything over that might endanger the plane."

"Oh, shut up! Screw the Operations Plan! The bloody book again!" Slattery shouted in exasperation. "There's too much book around here since you came aboard. By God, you don't think for a moment *Pickering* put up all those bursts by following the book. *Somerset*'s *not* going to be outshot."

"Captain, Mount Fifty-two reports trouble with the starboard stop. Shall I instruct them *not* to fire on the next run?" Ramsey had leaned perilously far out of the director to shout down his question. The starboard stop prevented the gun directly under the bridge from sluing all the way around and firing into the ship.

"No, by God," Slattery yelled back. "I want every gun shooting!"

That explains *Somerset*'s excellent gunnery record, Harry thought bitterly. Slattery cuts every corner. But using Mount Fifty-two could bring disaster upon them. The defective stop made it all the more imperative the destroyer cease fire within the safety angle. Harry's objections went unheard as Slattery rushed past him to the loudspeaker.

"Now hear this. This will be a firing run for *Somerset*. Extra liberty for the gun crew that brings down the target." Slattery snapped the mouthpiece back into place. "Two-block Baker," he roared to the quartermasters. This time the red flag went all the way up as the klaxon wailed again.

"Give me a bearing," Slattery ordered.

"I make the target thirty degrees off the bow, Captain. Another fifteen degrees to go."

"Like hell. Commence, commence, commence."

Wang-ohh. Mount Fifty-two fired first, followed by the rest of the ship's batteries in rapid succession. With a low moan, the young telephone talker ducked under the bridge rail. Paint flecks snowstormed the inside of the pilothouse. Harry heard crockery shatter belowdecks. His breath seemed squeezed from him as though he were clasped by a giant hand.

Wang-Ohh . . . Wang-Ohh. The guns were firing rapidly now, and suddenly no one cared about the muzzle blasts anymore. The waiting had been the worst part. In a line with, but slightly aft of, the target, *Somerset* put up the familiar row of small black dots against the blue sky. The muzzle blasts were suddenly distinctly louder as the forward guns trained aft in search of the elusive, skittering cylinder. Then the bridge no longer rocked to the worst of the pounding, and Harry realized that something was wrong. Mount Fifty-two wasn't firing. Almost in answer to his unspoken question, the talker, his eyes still glazed, screamed, "Hangfire in Mount Fifty-two!" The live round in the gun directly beneath them hadn't fired when the trigger was closed.

"Captain, the target is forty degrees off the beam now," Harry reminded Slattery. It did no good. The Captain was dancing with rage. The target was still up there. "Fifty degrees off the beam, Captain—five degrees past our safe limit," Harry argued.

"Oh, very well. They don't seem able to hit anything this morning anyway," grumbled Slattery. "Cease fire, cease fire, damn it all. Give me a bearing, Number One."

At this point all of the guns were in the stops except Mount Fifty-two, which continued to follow erratically as Dennis Ramsey slued the director farther aft. The starboard muzzle of the mount was by now practically touching the bridge just under where Harry stood. Instinctively, Harry bent over the pelorus to get Slattery's bearing, forgetting that the gun underneath him was still loaded.

The next minute Harry's world exploded into one monstrous orange-yellow flash, his feet went out from under him, and his steel helmet, the cloth strap torn clear through, went twenty feet up in the air. Dimly, Harry grasped the fact that he was now lying a good ten feet from where he had just been standing. Slowly he attempted to pull himself upright. A ragged cheering sounded all over *Somerset*. The last shot had cut the towplane cable, and Harry saw the red sleeve, looking like a crumpled sausage, plunge into the water. Then, mercifully, blackness set in, and he knew no more.

When Harry came to, he was on the wardroom couch, and Ted James was holding a vial of ammonia under his nose. Feebly, he pushed the ammonia away from the enormous clanging gong that seemed to be his head. Carefully he tested his extremities, pleased to find nothing broken. James's words seemed to come from afar. "You had us worried, Commander." Harry shook his head to show that he was all right, but he shook it very carefully indeed.

Twenty minutes later he was able to stand up, even to register the fact that the destroyer was now heading back toward the carrier. The slowly diminishing noise that seemed to float inside his skull was replaced by the pounding of the destroyer's narrow bows into the freshening seas. It had been a very narrow thing, he knew: another inch or so and the shell would have glanced off the bridge wing just where he stood. He knew something else, too. It had been Slattery who had ordered the unnecessary bearing from Harry, and it had been Slattery who had ducked inside the pilothouse at the last moment. He couldn't prove it, but Harry harbored a strong suspicion that Slattery had known all along what was going to happen. My God, Harry thought, either like Abel he was going insane, or Slattery was now trying to kill him.

"And this happened the day before Ensign James was washed overboard, Mr. Tolley?"

"Yes, sir."

"But I understood it was St. John who tried to rescue James. Your Executive Officer must have remarkable recuperative powers."

Give Hawk his due, thought Harry. The Trial Counsel was for a change trying to bring out something in his favor.

"It was because of St. John that poor Ted was lost in the first place," Paul Tolley suddenly blurted out.

"I see. You had better explain that."

Nine

The vessel creaked and groaned. From somewhere forward, an unsecured watertight door opened and closed with a monotonous loud clanging. An odor of unwashed bodies mixed with the ammonia stench of an overflowing urinal. Harry lay for a moment on the bunk, his stomach nauseated, his mouth furry, his head an all-encompassing burst of pain. He had had little sleep the night before, the effort of remaining in his heaving bunk making rest almost impossible. It was no small feat to brace oneself hours on end for the rise of the stern, the dizzying roll to port, the crash of the bows into green water.

Carefully timing his movements to the vessel's wild motion, Harry rose, climbed into oilskins, and worked his way topside to the bridge. They were far out into the Atlantic and heading east. East because dead ahead lay the first gray smudge of light. Far out because it was scarcely past five, and dawn would not come this early unless they were on the eastern fringe of the time zone.

The pilothouse crew carried out their duties with the leaden manner of sleepwalkers. In the light from the pilothouse he could see the rain driving aft in solid sheets. Enormous white-topped combers rose to starboard. The wind shrieked and moaned. He fought the ache in his head, the nausea in his stomach, and the stinging rain as he tried to remain vertical to the tilting, spinning horizon. Outside, a shadow moved across to the port pelorus. Hand over hand, St. John made his way to the Officer of the Deck.

Dennis Ramsey's fine Irish features streamed water, and coal-black hair plastered his forehead. "Three-zero-zero," he roared above the wind. "Right on station. Surprised to see you here after that clout yesterday."

Beyond Ramsey, Harry could see the great black bulk of *Argonne*. Twinkling lights to port marked the location of *Pickering*. Ramsey would be doing well to hold the destroyer within twenty degrees of station on a morning like this.

"Where's your Junior Officer of the Deck?" St. John had to make a megaphone of his hands in order to be heard. Ramsey thumbed aft to a moaning shadow that lay within the canvas cover of the flag bag.

"Seasick," Ramsey roared.

"I'll take his watch," St. John volunteered. "I can't sleep anyway."

James was rolling in his own vomit, his face green, his clothes filthy. "Ted, get below and get cleaned up," Harry bellowed.

"My watch," protested the feeble James.

"I'll relieve you. Get some rest."

He helped James out of the mess and sloshed out the signal bag with a bucket of salt water. Afterward, he located Ramsey in the comparative quiet of the pilothouse.

"Skipper been told it's making up?" It was a relief to talk in normal tones. Ramsey appeared amused by the question.

"Skipper doesn't know anything at the moment. He was down with the chiefs last night."

"What's that supposed to mean?"

Ramsey appraised him coolly before replying. "That means he and the chiefs got sloshed last night," he replied in even tones. "It's a Slattery tradition: a party for the chiefs every time we go to sea."

"Bridge, this is Combat Information Center." A red light on the pilothouse squawk box winked on and off. Harry thumbed down the switch. "Go ahead, Combat."

"Just got word from *Argonne*. All exercises are off this morning unless the weather gets better. They want to know how we're making out."

"Tell them, 'Just fine.' "

"Speak for yourself up there, Mr. James. I got a seasick crew, the Chief of the Watch ain't showed, and I'm up to my ankles in puke."

Dimly Harry recalled the name of the first-class radarman who had the morning watch. "This is Commander St. John. You're Perrelli, aren't you?"

"Yes, sir!"

"Well, Perrelli, you go down and get your Chief off his ass. I want him in Combat in ten minutes. Report back to me, *pronto*."

It was lighter now. With each wild rearing of the bows, Harry could see more shapes emerge from the racing foam. The jackstaff was canted at a crazy angle. The forward stanchions had been bent into insane patterns. Deck treads glued into place just before sailing were now all torn away. The canvas coverings over the breech mechanisms of the five-inch guns streamed wildly in tatters. Amidships, one splinter shield was caved in.

To port, *Pickering* was also making heavy weather of it. *Somerset*'s sister ship swam the heavy seas with the uncontrollability of a big log in wild surf. Twice a minute the destroyer's bow lunged clear of the waves, only to fall back again with magnificent pounding crashes. Vaguely Harry realized *Somerset* and her crew were taking a similar beating.

"Radio reports Washington acknowledged last night's outgoing, Mr. Ramsey," reported the bridge talker sleepily.

"Very well. Tell the quartermaster to enter that in the log."

"What's that all about?" St. John asked.

Ramsey grinned. "Skipper shot off a cable to Washington about the transfer of all coding material to you. He left orders the message be acknowledged and Washington's receipt entered in the log."

"What for?"

"Whatever his faults, Duke Slattery is a careful sonofabitch when it comes to sticking out his own neck. I suppose if any classified material gets lost, he wants it in the record you've got the bag. Thought you knew that!"

"I'm finding out more each day."

They passed the remaining hours of the watch without incident until the gray morning was well launched. At six thirty, in accordance with the Night Order Book, St. John went below to rouse Slattery.

The Captain lay in his bunk like a fallen oak, his mouth agape, his body swaying with the vessel's movements. He was naked except for grimy boxer shorts. There was an odor of whiskey in the small cabin. But even in this morning-after condition, Slattery's physical appearance was impressive. Beneath the coarse black hair that covered his body, bunched cords of muscles swelled and relaxed in harmony with the wild ride of the ship. A good man to have on your side in a bar fight, Harry conceded. Another surprise: Slattery awoke to the merest touch on his arm.

"What the hell is it?"

"Oh-six-thirty, Captain. Still heading east. Looks as though we're in for more dirty weather. Barometer fell another point last night. *Argonne* canceled all events."

"The fucking sweethearts—they give us the day off," he sneered. "Tell Willie I want coffee right away." His bloodshot eyes examined Harry. "How's the skull?"

"I'll live, Skipper." Then, with a contempt he didn't trouble to hide: "How's yours?"

"Wish I could say the same, Red Lead. You better believe it."

As Harry closed the door to Slattery's sea cabin, *Somerset* fell off into a trough and took an enormous roll to port. Amid the clatter of falling crockery and general cursing, Harry heard excited voices erupt on the Combat Information Center radio. He took the steps to the bridge two at a time, bursting into the pilothouse as *Somerset*'s whistle let go with an ear-rattling blast. The destroyer, aided by the wind and mounting sea, was in a sluggish left turn, her starboard rail full into the frothy surf. Ramsey clung to the port bridge rail.

"What the hell's going on?"

"*Argonne* reported seeing a man in the water. An officer. I think it's Ted."

"Oh, my God!"

They looked at each other, each knowing full well rescue in this sea was almost impossible.

"You wake the Skipper?"

"He's on the way. How about the carrier? You compensating?" Barely five hundred yards astern, *Argonne* pounded steadily forward, and then slowly started to come right in a surf-bursting turn. Signal flags erupted on her starboard yardarm as she told the formation she was maneuvering independently and her movements were to be disregarded. It was going to be a near, fine thing.

"That's far enough to port, Ramsey."

"Rudder amidships." Ramsey, quite pale, appeared on the verge of panic. His eyes beseeched Harry.

"You want me to take over?"

"I have the conn," boomed a familiar voice. Duke Slattery appeared behind the helmsman, clad exactly as Harry had last seen him. Shrugging off his jacket, Harry flung it to Slattery.

"I'll organize the rescue party," Harry volunteered, his words almost lost in a slamming burst of wind and spray.

But when Harry got to the windbreak, the half dozen deckhands milling about uncertainly were unequipped. Damn those drunken chiefs, he thought. There should be a line-throwing gun on hand, grapnels, heaving lines, a stretcher—all the rescue paraphernalia they practiced with. Even so, this was a near-impossible job. No one would want to go out on the heaving foredeck. But one man might be able to make it by going forward over the superstructure. With luck he could wedge himself under the jackstaff, ride the wildly submerging bow.

Harry bolted up the bridge ladder to the level directly above, grabbed a coil of heaving line from the bosun's locker, and a moment later had flattened himself against the port side of the superstructure. Below him, the deck was a maelstrom. Forward, and drawing rapidly ahead of the slowing destroyer, *Argonne* burst through enormous combers. For the moment, the carrier had flattened the seas directly in their path. He leaped for the deck and allowed the flood to push him forward into the eyes of the ship. Just in time, he locked both elbows around the bent stanchions as *Somerset*'s prow dug into another comber. Grimly he held on.

It was as though he were being dragged under by a submarine—like being keelhauled. On the second surfacing, he opened his eyes and scanned the angry sea ahead. *Somerset* was moving slowly through the patch of relatively calm water. If he were to find his shipmate, it would have to be here and on this one pass. Then he saw him.

The youngster was just to the left of *Somerset*'s bows. Blood streamed from his forehead. He was swimming with desperate energy for Harry, who readied the heaving line on his shoulder. The destroyer was downwind of James. Wind and sea would push him against the vessel—if Slattery simply held to the present course. Once against the vessel, James could haul himself aboard with the heaving line. The youngster had fantastic luck. All the wind and sea variables had canceled themselves out as *Somerset* had wallowed around into near-perfect rescue position.

Harry balled his fist around the lead weight of the heaving line. He felt *Somerset* shudder violently as Slattery backed down hard on both engines. Then the unexplainable happened. Somerset's bow wrenched to port, the cruel knife edge of the stem putting James on the starboard, or wrong, side. They were speeding up instead of slowing down. My God, they hadn't seen him.

Harry rolled over and faced the bridge. Oilskin-clad shapes dotted the bridge coaming like crows on a fence. He motioned desperately for *Somerset* to turn back to starboard. The wind flung back his curses unheard. The bridge crew seemed to ignore him. It was unreal, a nightmare. He rolled back and saw James sliding past the stem. He took quick aim, knowing he would have only one chance, and heaved the rescue line.

Ted James saw the thin line snake across the widening gap between him and *Somerset*. Then the line reached its full limit and tightened. It fell into the water a tantalizing four feet from him. He could almost reach it. But the lead weight that had taken the line there in the first place caused it to sink immediately. James's only hope went down with the line. With a tremendous effort, he cupped his hands and bellowed at Harry.

St. John saw the line sink and saw the widening gap between the helpless young officer and the destroyer. There would be no second chance. James's words had failed to reach him through the moaning wind. Then *Somerset*'s bow dug in once more. When Harry emerged, the Ensign was no longer in sight.

Ten

As Paul Tolley told his story, Christian Cutter, inconspicuously attired in civilian tweeds, leaned forward and listened carefully. The Vice Admiral sat in the back row of the little room, hidden behind the other spectators. He had more than a passing interest in this aspect of the investigation. He remembered well the night he had received the call from Newport.

When he had first received the news of Ensign James's death, Cutter had hung up the library phone and sagged weakly against the nightstand, a duodenal wrench of pain searing his insides. My God, James was dead! Until now, Cutter had controlled the *Somerset* operation, using his special authority as commanding officer of the project investigating the Truxton Ciphers compromise. But now the entire espionage community (Central Intelligence, the Defense Intelligence Agency, the Office of Naval Intelligence, Counterintelligence, etc.) would find their curiosity piqued and blunder into this mess. He had lost control. He stared at the mute telephone with disbelief.

He would have to leave that weekend and fly to Newport. He mopped his forehead, reassured by his foresight in making that lieutenant commander available for this final emergency. St. John would have to be told just enough about the Truxton Ciphers compromise so that he could testify for the Admiral in case anything went wrong. With great effort Cutter pulled himself together as his Filipino steward entered the library bearing a tray of after-dinner liqueurs.

"That will be fine, Diego. You may serve them now."

He followed Diego into the dining room of the fine old house he occupied on the grounds of the Naval Observatory and greeted his guests—two Senators from the Joint Committee on Armed Services.

"I must apologize, gentlemen," he greeted them. "These urgent calls in the evening are the curse of the workingman. Please help yourselves to the cigars—Philippine tobacco with Sumatra wrappers."

"No Cubans left, Admiral?" the elder Senator chided. He lifted a slim panatela from the cedar box proffered by the steward and rolled it appraisingly.

"Not until we redress that dismal foreign policy that was the subject of our dinnertime conversation, I'm afraid. But these are the next best thing. The seeds were smuggled from pre-Castro Cuba and now flourish in Luzon. If you like, I'll have Diego send you each a box."

"Thank you," said the younger Senator. He glanced about the elegant dining room with curiosity. "Quite frankly, I'm puzzled that a career bureaucrat would so readily go along with our argument. If we get you the C.N.O. job, it will of course mean your cooperation in cutting back the Fleet. Maybe even the end of accommodations such as these for admirals. Even though I'm a very inexperienced Senator," he said with a graceful bow to his colleague, "I'm already quite used to hearing the professional bureaucrat's bellow of outrage when his *raison d'être* is threatened."

"Where the greater good of the country is concerned, there can be no compromise, gentlemen."

It was a little too pious for the elder Senator. He was from the Midwest, and much less impressed with Cutter than his liberal colleague from New England. Like Cassius, he thought, this man has a lean and hungry look. "Dammit, Cutter, what worries me in what we are proposing, what amounts to drastically cutting into the Navy's budget, is that the other side appears to give us damned little encouragement. Aren't they even now expanding their naval activities all over the world—the Mediterranean, the Indian Ocean, the Caribbean, *our* very shores?"

Obviously irritated by that argument, the younger Senator tossed off his *fine* in one gulp. "If you'll forgive me, Senator," he interrupted. "The seas of the world are open to all. To say that you resent the intrusion of the Russian Fleet into those waters implies that for some strange reason you feel those waters are ours."

"Precisely," agreed Cutter, pleased that his argument had been made for him. He needed both their votes to clinch the job.

"Well, I don't wish to be known as the last Cold Warrior in the Senate, my friend. However, I submit that if we are successful in having our excellent host here tonight installed as Chief of Naval Operations next year, and if he carries out this program—mothballing of Polaris submarines, stoppage of new construction, the reduction of our permanent fleets around the world—there is going to be one hell of a vacuum into which the Russians just might move."

"Courage, my friend," the Admiral remonstrated gently. "I didn't win the Navy Cross without taking risks. I'm going along with your plan only because once the Russians realize what we're up to, I sincerely believe they will follow suit. But we'll take it step by step and see." There was no need to tell him that the younger Senator had agreed to support him for C.N.O. only if he backed the young New Englander's foreign-policy program.

And it was the younger Senator who sensed the most effective argument to sway his colleague. "Think of your taxpayers, Senator, who support a Navy that has yet to construct a single establishment in your state."

The older man wafted a smoke ring over the table. "My concern is with the defense of our country," he said slowly. "But in for a penny, in for a pound. When the times comes, you can count on me to help convince the President that Cutter's our man."

The couple occupied a window table at Gunder's, a turn-of-the-century New England farmhouse, now converted into a restaurant. Gunder's was magnificently situated at the top of several acres of prime farmland that had been rolled and seeded until the result was a magnificent greensward that sloped down to the wind-chopped waters of Narragansett Bay

Harry, dressed in his best blue uniform, still bore traces of his recent adventure on *Somerset*'s foredeck. One eye was badly swollen, and the bridge of his nose was covered with adhesive bandage. Still, the romantic courage of his nature, and the reminders of its physical cost, were not lost upon the girl. Somehow it fitted very well indeed with the navy blue serge, the thick bands of golden lace, and the small rainbow of service ribbons.

By contrast, the young WAVE officer looked stunningly unmilitary. She wore a close-fitting dress of pure cashmere, casual but elegant, its misty green-blue setting off her magnificent complexion. In her uniform, Diane had been merely an attractive girl; on this particular night she was a real beauty, or so she seemed to Harry. In fact, his shifting emotions of the moment were not entirely due to his past adventures; the girl had more than a little to do with his present state of confusion.

"It's hard to believe that it could happen. It seems like

only yesterday that Ted left our office to go to the ship. I remember how thrilled he was. It must have been terrible up there trying to rescue him. You never did tell me how you managed to get back after you lost sight of him."

He grinned ruefully. "I waited until the ship came up out of a big one, and then I let go. Half of the Atlantic fetched me aft. That's where all of this happened." He wigwagged a sore arm toward his battered features. "I had just about passed out when Chief Nielson caught me going over the side."

"And the day before, you think that someone ordered that last shot fired?"

"I *know* someone did."

"But how could a gun fire that close to the ship? I wish I could remember all of those things they taught us in officer candidate school. It isn't supposed to happen, is it?"

"No. I'll agree that it shouldn't happen. However, either that stop simply worked loose, or it was removed. That I don't know. But I do know that when I slid around behind the pelorus to get that last bearing, someone ordered that hangfire unloaded through the muzzle."

She looked confused. "But that would have to be the Gunnery Officer."

"No, Ramsey denied it, and I believe him. I also believe the gunner's mate when he told me that an order to unload through the muzzle actually came over the circuit."

"Who would be on the gunnery circuit then?"

Harry grinned sadly. "Half the ship, I'm afraid." Answering her puzzled look, he said, "I'm really no better off for my sore head than I was before it happened."

At that point his narrative was interrupted by the arrival of their waitress bearing a brace of succulent broiled lobsters. The shellfish had been taken from the sea just scant hours before cooking. Beneath the warm, rich butter, the tender flesh offered a salty aftertaste of the ocean, which they washed down with a sweet Pinot blanc. Diane watched Harry's face as he sketched in the remainder of *Somerset*'s cruise.

By late afternoon on the day James was lost, the storm abated. The crew of the destroyer found their vessel alone, the formation dissolved, the damaged vessels left to return by their own devices. *Spikefish,* the exercise submarine, had gone deep and far out into the Atlantic to escape the storm. With the ships thus dispersed, there was no way to restart the exercise without prior fueling and repairs.

Harry for one was glad of the respite. In addition to his other duties (which now included supervision of the repair work), he would have to see to it that Ted James's effects were shipped home, and a statement concerning his accidental drowning prepared. Also, there was the unhappy job of writing a letter to the boy's parents.

Slattery had remained on the bridge for the duration of the storm, which was fortunate, since it gave Harry time to calm down. He had been unable to save James and had nearly drowned himself. His first impulse had been to confront Slattery and accuse him of deliberately foiling the rescue attempt. Fortunately, he did not have the chance, for if Slattery had deliberately prevented James's rescue, and if the accident during the gunnery exercise had not been an accident at all, then Slattery was desperate. Harry would have to go after him with the caution one reserves for a wounded animal gone to ground.

Somerset was thirty miles from the mouth of Narragansett Bay and approaching Block Island. The seas were calm, the sky clear. Except for some additional damage to the motor whaleboat, the vessel appeared to be not much worse off than earlier in the morning.

By contrast, Duke Slattery appeared considerably improved. He strode the deck with bounce and energy, his eyes clear, his hand steady. Despite a day of extreme physical exertion, he appeared rested rather than exhausted.

He had cleaned up and changed into dress blues for the entrance into Newport, a smart-looking seaman bringing home his battered vessel. Unexpectedly, his eyes lit up at the sight of Harry.

"St. John, glad to see you're all right. The corpsman thought you might have broken a rib or two." Slattery's heavy arm slid reassuringly over Harry's shoulder. It was such an unexpected display of sentiment that it caught Harry off guard.

"A few bumps, Skipper. Nothing else."

"That was a mad, harebrained thing you did. I can't imagine how James could fall from the bridge."

"He wasn't on the bridge, Captain. I sent him below."

Slattery's astonishment appeared genuine. "But why?"

"Because he was seasick and totally unfit for duty. He couldn't stand his watch. I was trying to help."

"I'm sure you were." There was more than a faint edge of sarcasm to Slattery's tone.

"I almost had him, you know," Harry pressed. "If you had come right instead of going left, he might have made it."

"But man, we couldn't see him under the bows. You signaled to go left. Don't you remember? We thought you must have forgotten that you were facing aft."

Harry was astonished. So that was it. The way Slattery's report would come out, it would be Harry's fault, like so many other things that seemed to have happened since he had joined the ship. Harry fought the cold, sharp anger that rose within him. Before he could express his contempt, Paul Tolley stepped between the two of them. Beyond the Operations Officer, Dieter, the whaleboat coxswain, draped himself over the chart table.

"All set, Captain," reported Tolley.

"Coxswain, do you have room for a passenger?"

"Your boat, Captain," Dieter observed, his cold blue eyes

expressionless. He shrugged his shoulders to indicate his indifference.

"Okay, then." Slattery turned toward the lee helmsman. "All stop!"

With power off, the old destroyer glided closer inshore toward Block Island, until with an enormous ear-wrenching clatter, the anchor was let go. Shrieking gulls, disturbed by the roaring hawsepipe, soared from the island and quickly surrounded the vessel. As *Somerset* glided closer inshore, Slattery scanned the scrubby coast with powerful binoculars.

"I see a good spot, Dieter. I'll go with you and stretch my legs. Might even get in a little shooting." Slattery lit a cigar and drew in smoke with obvious relish. "St. John," he said, "I'm told the whaleboat's leaking like a sieve on the outboard side. Since Dieter can't get at it from the inside, he's going to beach and careen the boat. I'm going with him. We should return in a little over an hour. I'd like to head for home then."

"Why don't you wait and repair the boat in Newport, Captain?"

Slattery thrust forward a DesLant message. "We're to moor in the roadstead tonight. We'll need the boat when we get in."

"Fleet Boat Pool might provide us with one."

"We'll need a buoy party on arrival. I'm not taking the chance that some shore-duty idiot will see his way clear to do his duty, not when I can fix my own boat in an hour or so. Dieter tells me the boat should stay afloat until we get ashore. After that, it will be easy enough to patch her. I'm leaving you in charge, St. John."

Moments later, the little whaleboat, loaded with an extraordinary quantity of tools and equipment boxes, was lowered into the water. After a trial run around the destroyer to see that the bilge pump could cope with the leak, they set out for Block Island. Slattery, obviously as pleased as though he were a small boy on holiday, took the tiller himself. Evidently he found a satisfactory cove. The whaleboat, by then noticeably lower in the water, disappeared around a narrow spit of land. Shortly thereafter, they heard occasional bursts of small-arms fire as Slattery apparently succeeded in flushing game.

His temper cooled, Harry was in the process of leaving the bridge when he paused in front of the open door to the sonar room. The first-class sonarman, a grave young sailor, was just getting up from the video display. The glass was empty except for a small track of *XXX*'s south of where *Somerset* had anchored.

"Ears, I thought you had secured for the day."

"I did, Mr. St. John, but I wanted to check out the dome for storm damage."

"Everything okay?"

"Yeah; this old gear is pretty tough. I even picked up something just before we dropped the hook." He indicated the grease-pencil track. "Maybe *Spikefish* going home, or a whale. Hard to tell at this extreme range. In any case, the gear's okay." A fresh thought occurred to him. "But I do need a couple of good strikers, Mr. St. John. You know only one in five makes it through sonar school. I have to provide three for training now, but they aren't any good for anything except making coffee."

Harry smiled. He was growing very familiar with this request. Every division on the ship was shorthanded, and he had been deluged with requests for additional personnel since he started the training programs. Still, "Ears" was right; a good sonarman was the result of highly selective screening. Very few youngsters had the patience for the long hours on the scanning equipment, the intuition to select a hard contact from among a multitude of returns and the intellect to solve the intricate attack problem.

"I'll see what I can do for you, but I'm not promising anything."

Later, when it was too late, Harry was to recall that track of X's on which he now rested his hand.

"Weren't there any witnesses to contradict Slattery?" Diane asked the question as the Ford eased through black slush on Route 24, the road back to Newport.

"That's the funny part of it. All of the stories fitted perfectly, almost as though it was a conspiracy to back up Slattery. I know well enough that the Duke's enough of a seaman not to botch a rescue attempt like that. Yet no one but me seems to have the impression that he *did* botch it. Or if they do, they're afraid to say so."

"Harry, it sounds odd. Something's wrong on that ship, and you seem to be caught in the middle of it. I'm not sure that taking responsibility for the missing coding equipment was such a good idea. You gave Slattery a perfect out."

"Not while I'm still alive," Harry said grimly. "Enough sea stories. How was our Nation's Capital?"

"As always, it reminds me of a large, neat drugstore."

"*Alice in Wonderland*?"

She laughed. "There are moments down there when it does resemble the Mad Hatter's Tea Party."

"Still pretty impressive when you realize that the nerve ends reach all over the world, and you're in the brain."

"I had another part of the anatomy in mind," she said dryly.

He laughed, and the lamplight shone on his strong white teeth. He looks so battered, she thought; a misfit like myself. And he knew so little—a victim. She was sorry for him with his misplaced ideals.

"Did that fairy flag officer go with you?"

"Yes. He kept making passes all the way down."

"Passes? Him?"

"Oh, not at *me*. A large, fat businessman complete with toupee and snap-lock briefcase took an interest in me. I enjoyed being the bait. Poor Lashes played his little pathetic game all the way down. They left me at the airport arm in arm; the corporate industrialist was promised an evening in a naval Sodom and Gomorrah. If he gets drunk enough and the room is dark enough, he might even go along with Lashes."

"Hey, there are certain basic differences."

"I guess if you're drunk enough it doesn't matter. At least, I think that's what Lashes hopes."

The bitterness in her voice surprised him. "You sound pretty cynical."

"I think I'm just being realistic. People can be rotten sometimes."

"Does that apply to me?"

"You're different."

"A kind of mutilated charm—like Nelson?"

Yes, she thought the comparison was fair. She thought she could see why Emma Hamilton might risk losing the British Ambassador to Naples.

Harry eased the Ford into the parking apron behind officers' quarters and switched off the engine. It was Sunday night, and the lot was deserted except for an occasional look-in by the Shore Patrol. Chill air crept into the car the moment the heater was turned off. She started to open the car door, but he caught her by the hand.

"Can I come up?"

She regarded him gravely. "No, I think not. You're too dangerous."

"You can always yell for a steward."

She laughed. "No, not dangerous in that way. I've coped with *that* for a long time. I mean, you rouse sentiments in me that I'd prefer not to have—for both our sakes."

Her remark puzzled him. "You mean I don't fit into your

master plan, with my come-and-go life. Maybe if I got transferred ashore . . ."

". . . You'd be miserably unhappy."

". . . But you'd be worth it."

She laughed. "No, Harry, I need a little more time." She leaned across and placed a small finger on his lips. "I'm not that casual. If you want us to be lovers, I need time to decide."

Then, quite unexpectedly, they were illuminated in the glare of a flashlight. Harry recorded a brief impression of astonishment on the girl's face, until she screened those incredible blue-green eyes behind her lashes and turned away. Outraged at this affront to their privacy, he swung around quickly. Behind the flashlight, which now bobbed up and down, Harry recognized one of the B.O.Q. stewards.

"Miss Halliday? Mr. St. John?"

"That's right. What the hell is this?"

"Dunno, sir. I was told to look for you. There's an admiral inside waiting for you."

"An Admiral!" Diane exclaimed. "Harry, what in the world. . . ?"

"Must be your friend Cutter. He's got a great sense of timing. Diane, did you know anything about this?"

"Of course not. I've never even met the man."

As they followed the steward into the building, she explained further. "The only communication with him that we ever had was a brief memorandum concerning you. He asked that your inventory report be transmitted to him directly, rather than through channels."

"What an odd request. Was it?"

"Harry, he's a Vice Admiral. Of course it was."

They found Cutter in the small downstairs lounge of V.I.P. quarters. Submerged in a green leather armchair, he had fashioned an impromptu desk by resting a worn attaché case on his lap. He was hard at work. A small charcoal fire burned in the grate before him, lending a domestic touch to the otherwise characterless room. Cutter seemed genuinely pleased to see them. He rose from his chair and peered over the tops of his Ben Franklin glasses.

"Miss Halliday, it's a great pleasure to meet you at last. Among other things, I owe you my thanks for so quickly reporting what Commander St. John discovered on his ship."

"You're more than welcome, sir." It amused St. John to note that the girl had fully recovered her composure and was not disturbed one whit by this encounter with the prestigious Admiral.

"And you, St. John. You look fit despite your recent adventures."

"Thank you, sir."

"I really must apologize for this interruption in your evening. I had to see you, St. John, and since I was in Boston on business, I thought I might kill two birds with one stone."

"How did you find me?"

"Your Commanding Officer was most helpful. Yes, most helpful indeed. Ah, Miss Halliday, I'm afraid that I must preempt the next hour. It's a matter of some urgency, or I wouldn't dare impose in this manner. I wonder if on your way out, you would be kind enough to ask the steward to bring me a glass of my usual sherry. It was a drafty ride up from Washington on that airplane, and I'm afraid these old bones have begun to feel their age. Commander, what would you care for?"

Hell's fire, thought Harry; the evening that had begun so promisingly was now ruined. But there was little he could do about it. Although he was sorely tempted, one can't very well tell a vice admiral to buzz off. "Scotch on the rocks will do nicely, sir," he finally replied. He turned to Diane. "May I call you tomorrow?"

"Yes, please do. I'll be on duty till noon. Good night, Admiral."

While they waited for the steward with their drinks, Cutter assembled the papers in his lap. "Commander, would you please be so kind as to poke up that small excuse for a fire?"

When Harry had done what he could, the steward returned with their drinks. Admiral Cutter handed him a generous tumbler, smiled pleasantly, and hoisted his own glass. "Shipmates, past and present," he offered. The Admiral then began without further prelude.

"Young man, I hope you are familiar enough with current events to know that I have recently taken a stance with regard to our ballistic-missile submarine fleet—a stance that is somewhat at odds with the present position of the naval establishment. Partially as a result of this somewhat outspoken position of mine, I have been reassigned to another project. That project concerns counterintelligence. I am, in fact, in charge of a small workshop that has only one objective, the tracing down of what appears to be a persistent compromise of one of our important coding systems."

Harry whistled softly and raised an eyebrow.

"You may well register surprise, Commander," pursued the Admiral. "It's a nasty business. We have known for some time that a leak exists. God knows we have changed the particular system often enough in the past two years." Absently, he studied the amber tones of the Dry Sack, twisting the stem of the crystal so as to elicit delicate hues and subtle shadings on the cut-glass edges. "Of course, the question is: how to find the source. In the past it would have been difficult enough to investigate such a crime. However, one could at least start with certain 'givens'—the reliability of our officer corps, for example. Today I no longer believe this is true."

"And you limit the hunt to the United States? It could be a treaty-organization recipient," Harry volunteered.

"No, Commander, we can rule out that theory. All of the treaty organizations—NATO and SEATO, for example—have their own allowances and some of our own nonsensitive codes as well. The Bloc seems to have acquired free access through Class Four—the Truxton Ciphers."

Harry was impressed by the gravity of what the old man had just told him. Class Four reached all the way through the fleet. Thanks to NASA press announcements, Cape Kennedy launchings invariably included Russian trawlers with elaborate snooping apparatus. However, lately such trawlers had appeared at routine fleet operations, drawn as if by an enormous magnet from far across the ocean to play a complicated game with U.S. forces. Worse yet, as in any big bureaucracy, units of the fleet exchanged an enormous communications traffic on a multitude of sensitive subjects. In the hands of experienced intelligence experts, a few months' accumulation of this traffic would provide a wealth of classified information.

"Perhaps their computers are breaking our systems as fast as they're changed," Harry volunteered.

Cutter looked pained. "No, Commander. Our experts tell us that it would take several years for their computers to resolve all of the possible combinations and permutations."

"Perhaps several computers could break the system in less time," Harry suggested, not to be daunted by the technical turn of the discussion. It was a mistake.

"The input to one problem depends on the output from the previous solution. One or a million computers, the result would be the same. No, Commander—it's a leak, all right, by person or persons unknown. We have known about it for some time." He paused and emphasized his next words. "Now, we *may* know the source."

Harry straightened in his chair.

"Some weeks ago, a Gloucester trawler picked up the body of a drowned officer. The officer happened to be carrying one of the Class Four rotors in his pocket. That rotor had been reported as destroyed some weeks ago."

"That was Abel?" A blind shot, but right on target.

"Yes, that was Abel, who may yet have served his country well. Because it is highly unusual for an officer to deliberately falsify an inventory report, we put an operative aboard your ship right away. It was a routine precaution, but we also had the faint hope that we might have found our leak at last. However, there could be a hundred explanations for a missing rotor. We would have to be absolutely certain before we could take any action at all." Cutter paused in order to emphasize his next words. "*Ensign Edward James, a highly skilled cryptoanalyst, was our operative.*"

"But James was a kid!" Harry exploded. "By God, I myself had to give him lessons in cryptographic procedures only last week."

"I would very much like to have seen that, Commander," the old man continued dryly. "Ensign James had a doctoral degree in mathematics and had developed some highly original work in cuing theory with random occurrences. For two years he did invaluable work for the National Security Agency on Bloc coding systems. He apparently had some theatrical talents as well."

"But why did you let him go?"

The old man sighed sadly. "He was a romantic—he wanted adventure. And he was persistent. It was a major blunder on my part."

"Where did I fit in?"

"You were simply to be a distraction from James's arrival on board, and a lifeline in case you were needed by James. Since you were a fresh replacement, we knew that we could trust you. Think back, Commander: did James tell you anything—anything at all—before he was swept away?"

"No, sir," Harry admitted sadly. "Up there on the foc'sle, I couldn't hear a word."

"I'm afraid that's not much help, then, Commander."

"No, sir. But if James and Abel were both deliberately done in, then you must be getting close to something."

"Yes—and if we *are* getting close, then of course James had to go." The Admiral paused and smiled wanly at Harry. "You, of course, have now become the prime threat to our man."

"You mean I may now be the one to be in danger," Harry replied, thinking of his own experience during the gunnery shoot.

"Precisely. That is why I thought it best to tell you all of this. You can well believe me when I say that you are up against a cunning and desperate man."

"Can you tell me whom you suspect?"

Admiral Cutter turned up both palms as he shrugged his shoulders. "That's the trouble—we have no suspect. I would suppose that Ted James could have given us the answer. I'm afraid that we have no choice now but to count upon you for the answer to that question."

Some two miles away, as Harry and the Admiral spoke, *Somerset*'s Supply Officer finished his carry-forward of the destroyer's cash accounts for another week. The Supply Officer was worried. Stacked before him in neat bundles of twenties lay an even fifty thousand dollars—more money than Poindexter had ever before seen.

The money represented *Somerset*'s payroll requirements for the next six months. Normally, Poindexter, as meticulous with his accounts as an Internal Revenue auditor, kept no more cash on hand than one extra payroll for emergencies. However, earlier that week, *Somerset*'s Commanding Officer had cornered him in the Supply Office, ordered out the storekeepers, and closed the door.

Slattery had forced Poindexter to fill out the requisition for an allotment of additional funds right then and there. Slattery hadn't volunteered an explanation, and Poindexter, who had only one more month to serve aboard the destroyer, hadn't cared to push his reluctance too far.

"I *will* need some reason, though," he protested nervously. "This is a bigger disbursement than any destroyer has a reason to request. DesLant is bound to be curious."

"Goddamn it, I didn't make the Operating Schedule. Tell them to check with NavOps if it worries them."

"You mean that we might go on extended cruise after Iron Strike?" Poindexter's concern had now shifted from the excess cash to his own imminent transfer to shore duty. The vision of the small furnished apartment that he had carried in his mind's eye during the past awful year seemed to swim before him. It would be just his luck to get held up aboard this hell ship for another few months. Slattery had had to use only a small distortion of the truth to get what he wanted.

"Pay, in this man's navy, you never know, do you? But if we are detached from Iron Strike and sent on extended cruise without payroll funds, you'll certainly have to remain aboard, won't you? I mean, a storekeeper would not be bonded to draw the cash."

"I'll take care of it, Skipper." Most reluctantly, Poindexter took the disbursement request and signed it.

"One last thing, Paymaster," Slattery continued. "Tomorrow I'll need a cashier's check for three thousand dollars from my personal account."

"Easy enough, Captain. I can make it out tonight if you wish." Poindexter lifted an eyebrow. "That's a large amount, though—practically all the cash I'm holding for you."

"I know. There's no hurry. Have it delivered to me before we sail."

"Whom shall I make it out to?"

"This outfit." Slattery proffered a small slip of paper to the Supply Officer. "I'm buying into one of these research deals with tax-free interest income," he said casually.

On the embossed letterhead of the paper, Poindexter read: FOUNDATION FOR THE ADVANCEMENT OF INTERNATIONAL NON-THEATRICAL EVENTS.

Eleven

It was shortly past noon when Harry presented himself at the counter of the Operations Center.

"Lieutenant Halliday just left," the duty yeoman grumbled.

"Did she say where she was going?"

"Uh . . . into town, I think." He stabbed a finger in the direction of the window. "Look, there she goes now!"

Harry saw a little red Fiat trailing a plume of condensed vapor zip round the corner and disappear over the hill leading to the main gate. "Thanks," he shouted over his shoulder. He quickly retraced his steps to the Ford and, draping the ice skates over the front seat, switched on the engine and set off in pursuit.

Once on the highway, he resisted the temptation to floor the throttle. Newport was a small town, and sooner or later he would have to overhaul her. It had been a bad week so far, and a traffic ticket would not improve his disposition. In fact, this last-ditch effort to organize an impromptu skating date was an outgrowth of an otherwise lonely six days. Slattery had availed himself of a chance to take a one-week officers' command course at the War College, and Harry had been left in charge of the old destroyer as a sort of resident housekeeper. It was dull work. Further, there was Cutter's stunning supposition to brood upon, a supposition that effectively precluded confidence and therefore companionship on any satisfactory level. Harry's resultant aloofness was misinterpreted by his messmates as new evidence of his lack of appreciation of their efforts. Some wag (he suspected Tolley) had even left a bit of scholarly nonsense on his desk.

> We trained hard, but it seemed that every time we were beginning to form up into teams, we would be reorganized. I was to learn later in life that we tend to meet any new situation by reorganizing, and a wonderful method it can be for creating the illusion of progress while only producing confusion, inefficiency, and demoralization.
>
> Petronius Arbiter, A.D.66

By Saturday morning Harry realized that he would be much the better for a few hours off the ship. "Hebrews thirteen," he muttered to himself. "Jesus Christ the same yesterday, and today, and forever." Or so it seemed to him.

He almost missed the Fiat. Cutting back between Thames and Coggeshall avenues, he slowed up for a neighborhood touch-football match. Glancing around to make sure that the last of the ten-year-olds was out of his way, he spotted the Fiat parked down a side street. He cut hard left and parked behind her. Hobson's choice. There was only one commercial activity as far as he could see: an ancient, sagging structure, whose rotting wood appeared held together by a coat of peeling gray paint. He mounted tottering wooden steps and confronted a glistening brass plaque that announced the FOUNDATION FOR THE ADVANCEMENT OF INTERNATIONAL NON-THEATRICAL EVENTS.

An old-fashioned shop bell tinkled as he opened the door. There were only two people in the office. Diane was caught off guard, and her hand flew to her cheek in amazement. "Harry—was I supposed to meet you?"

"No. I just had a silly idea and wanted to see you. I happened to be behind your car as you came into town."

A soft pinkness worked its way into her face, the skin creamy as the top of a strawberry soda. "Oh, I see. Well, I won't be but a minute. Harry, I'd like you to meet Mr. Meek. Mr. Meek, Commander St. John."

A gaunt specter of a man rose from behind the only desk in the room. Mr. Meek's few remaining strands of hair were pasted across his scalp in a MacArthur-like attempt at creating the illusion of youth. Beneath an enormous forehead, Meek's nose turned upward to such a degree that it presented rather more of his nostrils than one cared to see. A nervous tic pulled at the corner of his mouth as his eyes took in Harry in a single glance.

"So pleasant to make your acquaintance, Commander."

After Mr. Meek's talonlike fingers had been released from Harry's hearty grasp, he proceeded to dry wash them. An aroma of bad breath emerged between the two of them like a bubble bursting from a stagnant sewer. Harry backed away quickly. "So sorry to interrupt," he said, a trifle desperately. He glanced around the dingy, dirty little office. "I can wait outside, Diane, until you're free."

"Oh, no," the girl said with a smile. "Mr. Meek has requested our cooperation in permitting a fund-raising campaign to be carried out on the naval base. I simply wanted to get further information from him before a decision is made." She waved a sheaf of brightly colored folders in the air. "I really think I have everything I need now."

"Fund raising?" Harry's confusion was evident, and Mr. Meek was only too happy to come to the rescue.

"Ah, yes, Commander," he purred. "You see, the Foundation—nonprofit and tax-deductible, of course—attempts to promote what we consider to be the many worthwhile efforts of our global community to develop a healthy harmony with nature, while at the same time achieving modest economic progress. You will of course recall the World Weather Watch Program recently carried out by several governments. We participated in that program in a modest but meaningful way. This year the emphasis is on the exploration of the sea bottom—the mining of the vast resources of the deep, as it were." A look of pure panic crossed Harry's face, and Meek, sensing he was losing his audience, was quick to press home his point. "Even though we are supported by various worthy organizations, there still exists a distressing lack of capital." He drew closer. "If you feel as though a personal investment might be in order . . ." He pressed several leaflets into Harry's hand.

"Yes . . . yes, of course." Harry yanked open the door as he coughed into his handkerchief. Mr. Meek's hand clamped upon his paper collar as a heaven-sent shaft of fresh air struck them. "Almost any amount would be satisfactory," Mr. Meek suggested wildly as Harry bolted through the door with Diane.

Outside, Harry shuddered with relief. "Good Lord, what a disgusting person," he said as he tossed the brochures into a trash bin.

Diane laughed. "Oh, he's really not so bad. We get a lot of such screwball inquiries. They all have to be run down and answered."

"You must have a martyr complex," he observed. "Any moment in there I expected an organ to start playing, and Mr. Meek to inquire if we wanted to view the body. I never heard such rot in my life."

"Oh, come on, now. He was just trying." They stopped at Harry's car. "What did you want to see me about?"

"From the ridiculous to the sublime. I wanted to ask you if you wanted to go ice skating." He reached into the car and held up the shining ice skates as one would use dime-store jewelry to tempt a little girl.

Her eyes widened with pleasure. "Harry, what a splendid idea! But where?"

"You don't know anything about life, do you? You wait for a cold day like this and then simply follow the first kid you meet carrying a pair of skates. You needn't worry—I only take you to the best places."

And it was just that simple. The "best place" turned out to be a small pond located just inside the woods at the bottom of Greenend Avenue.

An hour later, Harry relaxed and stretched his legs toward the small wood fire he had built on the edge of the pond. The winter sun shone brightly, the odor of burning wood hung pleasantly on the late-noon air, and the cold sea before them broke languidly upon the shore. He lit a cigarette from a twisted twig and offered it to Diane. She declined the offer, but moved a fraction of an inch closer and slid her arm through his. It was a gesture that he found particularly pleasant.

"I'm impressed," the girl confessed over a mug of wardroom stoneware. "A mere commander who both consorts with famous admirals and produces a thermos of coffee on a cold afternoon can't be all bad."

"Watch that *mere*-commander bit," he cautioned. "Impressionable you, that was the general idea when I invited you out to this Currier-and-Ives setting."

"And it is just that delightful," she agreed. "How ever did you escape from Slattery's clutches this time?"

"Piece of cake. He, along with every senior officer in Newport this afternoon, is swilling down free liquor at a staff luncheon. I just hope he stays sober."

"Harry, if he's the sort you say he is, don't the other officers know it?"

"Diane, that's the funny part. Dressed to the nines, Duke Slattery is *impressive*." Harry recalled the sight of his Commanding Officer that morning as Slattery had stepped across the gangway to the rattle of his absentee pennant soaring to the yardarm. Gone were the filthy fisherman's waders, replaced by expensive, well-buffed oxfords. The prison haircut was hidden under a starched and spotlessly white cap cover from which sprouted the golden leaves of full-commander rank. The coarse, heavy frame disappeared beneath Slattery's tailored number-one blues, and the cloth draped elegantly from his impressive height. No, dressed for the part, every inch of Slattery bore the stamp of order, dedication, and disciplined effort leading to command responsibility.

"Well, I'm sure that one day the Navy will catch up with him." She gave Harry's arm a loyal squeeze. "Perhaps the brass will size him up correctly at this luncheon, and you'll find yourself in command of *Somerset*."

"A lot of people suspect me of wanting that right now."

"And do you?"

He laughed. "Frankly, yes. But not at the expense of Slattery, as much as I may dislike him."

"Harry, may I ask what's behind all of this: Cutter's trip up here, your call to me that first night, the missing coding equipment, and James's disappearance?"

"No, you may not ask. On the other hand, I'm pleased that you're curious."

"Why are you pleased?"

"Because that tells me that you, at least, aren't involved."

"Harry!"

"I thought you might even have some answers for me. For instance, if I may use the expression, what's a good-looking broad like you doing in the WAVES in the first place?"

"That sounds suspiciously like a variation on the question men are supposed to ask whores."

"You know I didn't mean it that way."

"I know you didn't. The answer's simple enough. I lost my dad in the Second World War—Atlantic convoy duty in 1942. He was a lot like you. My sisters and the other officers' wives took care of my mother until I was old enough. I did my share and then left home. There's nothing sadder than a woman with a bottle talking about things that happened ten years before. I had no other place to go. You see, I'm like you: the Navy is my home too. Pretty silly for a girl, I guess."

"No, there's nothing silly about it. But you're unusual—like a composite of a *Playboy* centerfold and a recruiting poster."

She laughed. "Uncle Sam Wants You?"

"In your case, I suspect it's more like the whole fleet wants you."

She smiled and said softly, "No woman can resist that approach." She put her hand on his arm. "This conversation isn't fair. You have a few skeletons too. I heard something about a minesweeper."

His eyes told her that the wound had never fully healed. She prompted: "Her name was *Yellowbird*, and you lost her?"

"Yes, a long time ago—at Wonsan—with practically all the crew."

"Do you want to talk about it?"

"There's nothing to say." No, he thought, that's not true. But how can one describe the smell of cordite floating on the thin cold air, the shattering blasts of the salvos fired all around them as fast as the fleet could load and lock; and how could anyone be made to feel that moment of special horror when the ugly, rust-streaked Russian-built mine bobbed to the surface directly in their path?

"Wasn't there some sort of investigation?"

"Yes."

"I was told it wasn't really your fault."

"It's always someone's fault when a ship is lost. But since you asked, the sweeper to starboard fouled my gear. I took a chance and pulled out of the swept channel to clear it."

"And the court didn't understand that?"

He laughed bitterly. "Oh, yes, they understood. There was a short written statement and an interview with three extremely sympathetic gentlemen. Everyone understood. The trouble came three months later when I received an official reprimand for poor judgment, and as punishment, the loss of one hundred signal numbers. A sort of naval kiss-of-death."

"And then . . ."

"And then the worst assignments anyone ever had."

"Until this one."

"Yes, until this one." He glanced at his watch. "Well, you have heard the exile's tale. Now what do you say to a hot buttered rum at Gunder's?"

"Oh, I couldn't possibly go there looking like this."

"Well, then?"

"Would you settle for some bourbon at my place?"

He grinned. "I thought you'd never ask."

Diane's room at the B.O.Q. was a jumble of dreary Danish Modern furniture, art books strewn carelessly about, an ironing board set up in the corner, and a small dry-sink bar. A Hogarth print relieved the monotony of travel posters Scotch-taped to the wall. In the bedroom, a bra dangling from the lampshade hinted of other attractions.

"I'm afraid it's a mess."

"No. It's just comfortable. I like the Hogarth. How ever did you talk the Navy into a suite?"

"Oh, nothing dramatic. My tour here is to run for four years, so I was entitled to it. Anyway, I'm glad you like things homey." The blue-green eyes appraised him coolly. "There's liquor in the dry sink, but I don't think I have Scotch or rum. Help yourself. I'm getting out of these damp clothes."

While she went into the bedroom, St. John found bitters, bourbon, and a jar of cherries. With indifferent skill he mixed together the ingredients of a pair of Old Fashioneds. Searching for a stirrer, he pawed through a small drawer that apparently contained only kitchen linens. But the drawer wouldn't shut, and he had to yank it open again. The linen was bunched up on the end because a small medicine bottle had rolled forward under the dish towels. He turned the bottle over in his palm and read the prescription: TUINAL/1.5 GRAINS/100. USE AS DIRECTED. The bottle of sleeping pills was half empty.

At that moment Diane stepped out of the bedroom. Her transformation to thin white blouse, worn without bra, and miniskirt changed his entire line of thought. Purposefully she came to him and removed the bottle from his hand. From her manner, there could be no mistaking her mood. "We can have a drink later," she said, every word a silken invitation. He placed his arms around her slim waist and drew her to him. She smiled and went with him to the bedroom.

At that same moment, a few miles away, the petty officer in charge of *Somerset*'s Control Center had much the same idea on his mind. In addition to his skill at solving the intricate maneuvering problems of the old destroyer, Spider Perrelli was generally regarded by the ship's company as being an ass man *extraordinaire*. His success in this important area was due to two things: one, he approached the whole subject of fornication with the zeal of a missionary converting pagans; and two, when he was high on booze or a "joint," he could outdance the entire Atlantic Fleet.

Perrelli was, in fact, a born hoofer. He could improvise steps that would baffle a whirling dervish. When the Spider was at work on a dance floor, girls tended to overlook the swarthy complexion, the heavy black brows that joined over his nose, and the overoiled, overlong, coal-black mane of which he was so vain. On the contrary, when the jukebox started, Spider was six feet tall, with legs like Sammy Davis, Jr.'s. He moved with a grace that flowed uninhibited through three generations of Sicilian *tarantellisti*. Girls from Pearl to Norfolk counted it a real challenge to keep up with him. But dancing just set the scene, he knew, and before the euphoria wore off it was important to press home his advantage. That was why the Spider was at this very moment trying to work one hand up between the thighs of the perspiring girl who now sat beside him in a booth at Newport's White Hat Club.

"Don't!" pouted the girl sharply. She backed into her corner. "I told you, I have an escort." Perrelli caught her hand and forced it over the immensity between his legs.

"Gloria, baby," he pleaded. "I got the 'hots.' We were so great together last time."

"No," the girl protested, almost swallowing her gum at the sensation of Perrelli's manhood in full erection. She yanked her hand from between his locked thighs.

"You swabs are all the same," she complained. "That's all you want off a girl. You never think of anything but the next port and the next girl."

This was a familiar complaint. Perrelli flared his nostrils and hooded his eyelids as he had once seen Marcello Mastroiani do in a similar situation. The result was more than absurd; it was comic. Gloria stifled a laugh, but at the same time she was vaguely touched.

"You know, baby, just as soon as I make chief," he pleaded. The girl started to reply and then stared over his shoulder in annoyance. Perrelli heard approaching footsteps and then felt that same shoulder suddenly squeezed in a clasp of extraordinary power. Helpless, he was spun around to confront the unsmiling face of Dieter, *Somerset*'s coxswain.

"Get outa here, Wop," the coxswain commanded. "I gotta date with this broad."

In truth, Perrelli was somewhat less than courageous, but in front of a woman it was a different matter. He measured the dumb, unsmiling face of Dieter, sensed the power in the oxlike frame, but still felt the affront to heritage and manhood too monstrous to go unchallenged.

"Who you calling Wop, you dumb Polack bastard?" His *élan* was as untimely as the French cavalry charge at Waterloo.

For answer, the stocky coxswain chopped once, hard, across the bridge of Spider's nose with an axlike open hand. Perrelli felt the bone break. There was a sharp stab of pain, and crimson gushed forth over his best tailor-made blues. With an outraged bellow, Perrelli was up and out of the booth. Dieter backed away, contemplating the radarman with a cold air of amusement. Tables cleared instantly from around the combatants, and the bartender picked up a sawed-off baseball bat. With a bored yawn, the cashier rang up the Shore Patrol.

The first round went to Perrelli. A quick feint with those flying feet, and the Spider sank his fist deep into Dieter's Adam's apple. It was the kind of fast, lucky punch that had once before spelled success for the radarman. But not this time! Dieter only grunted and stepped back. His eyes misted momentarily. Then he came on.

Backed into a corner and raining blows on the flat, featureless face, Perrelli felt short, powerful arms lock behind his back. Seemingly without effort and oblivious of the radarman's frantic flurry of short-range punches, Dieter simply lifted Perrelli off his feet and bent him over backward. There was a white flash of incredible pain, and then Spider felt the first rib break. Perrelli had once read a magazine article concerning torture devices used by the Spanish Inquisition. The story claimed that once a victim was stretched upon the delicate machinery of the *cama de verdad,* his ribs could be shattered by the merest brush of a feather. In this incredible grasp of Dieter's, he could well believe that the tale was true. Feebly, he aimed a knee toward Dieter's groin. The man simply grunted. A beer bottle, hurled from somewhere, crashed against Dieter's skull. The pressure continued unabated. As his second rib snapped, Perrelli saw, through the red fog now beginning to envelop him, an S.P. brassard. He heard the swish and felt the breath of a descending nightstick. Then, mercifully, Perrelli collapsed.

Diego braked the car to a smooth, swooping stop before one of those impossible traffic signs at Dupont Circle that invariably baffle those unfamiliar with the traffic patterns of Washington, D.C. With satisfaction, Cutter noted that Diego had found the inner artery that enabled them to proceed along Massachusetts Avenue. It had been a long and eventful day, climaxed by a reception given by the new Chilean Ambassador to Washington. The Ambassador, concerned lest his new President's action with regard to the nationalization of the American copper mines be misinterpreted, had conspicuously invited the American military establishment to his party, both to hopefully sample opinion then current among the Joint Chiefs of Staff and to signal Chile's peaceful intention to remain friends with powerful right-wing elements in the United States.

As expected, the subtle Chilean wines had worked their magic. When the Ambassador's wife, an elegant blond *señora* several years younger than the Ambassador, had led an impromptu guitar and song fest, Cutter had been amused to note the warm sentiments evoked from among the most extreme elements of the Yankee generals and admirals gathered around her in open admiration. For a few moments even Cutter had been able to forget his nagging concern over the affair at Newport.

The car now sped rapidly up Massachusetts Avenue past the Fairfax Hotel, of Jackie Kennedy fame, and the copper-roofed embassies of the world's most powerful nations. By the time Diego had driven through the deserted gateway to the Observatory and pulled into the driveway of the Admiral's fine old house, Cutter found himself still unwilling to yield up the peaceful evening.

"Put the car in the garage, Diego, and turn down my bed. I'll be in the garden for a few moments."

The Admiral lit one of his Tabaceleras and lofted a perfumed halo of cigar smoke upon the night air that held the promise of spring. In a few weeks the first of his prize flowers would bloom and he would be able to see the results of his efforts of the fall. He was bending over his azaleas when he became aware that he was no longer alone.

"Who's there?" he barked.

A shadow detached itself from a corner of the house and moved toward him. Then the clouds parted and a beam of moonlight shone full on Meek's features.

"You must be insane to come here like this," Cutter hissed.

"It couldn't be helped. Something happened early this afternoon that will accelerate our planning. I flew down right away. Where can we talk?"

For answer Cutter stepped through the garden and unlocked the sliding doors of his small den on the ground floor. "Quick, in here! If you are seen, I'll have a hard time explaining this visit."

When they were at last alone in the small room with the curtains drawn, Cutter, white-faced and visibly shaken, quickly poured out two cognacs.

"I had a visit from your Commander St. John this morning," Meek began flatly after gulping down the *fine*.

"He knows nothing."

"Then what was he doing there?"

Cutter held up his hand. "No, no! St. John is only a pawn in this game. I selected him myself for what we have in mind. He's not an intelligence officer."

"I hoped you would say that, Admiral."

"Of course. But I can see how you would feel about it. Now where do we stand?"

Meek glanced at his watch. "We should have carried out the first step by now."

"Excellent."

"Admiral, I'm still troubled over whether or not we have this authority."

"My dear Meek, the arrangement was clear from the start. We were not to risk discovery. I will take full responsibility. Now here is what I want you to do. . . ."

Twelve

"And so you finally sailed without your leading radarman, Mr. St. John?"

"Yes, sir."

"As Executive Officer, did you try to get a replacement?"

"No, sir. The Captain said it was too late, to forget it."

Hawk lifted an eyebrow. "He did? How strange."

Not strange at all. Not strange if you knew Slattery.

Harry found Slattery in his untidy shore cabin, immersed in the Iron Strike operations folder. The steward fluttered over him, making halfhearted attempts to restore order. "Get the hell outta here, Willie," Slattery growled. "Here, deliver this!" He gave Willie a small slip of paper. "Okay, Number One, what's your complaint this time?"

The Captain chuckled when he heard the news. "Sounds like a great scrap, Red Lead. Always tell a good crew by the way they don't take any crap ashore."

"They weren't fighting for the ship. They were fighting each other. Dieter is a real troublemaker."

"Where have you been, Red Lead? I'd rather have them

mix it up ashore than aboard. A sailor ashore has to get it out of his system. Leave Dieter to me."

Harry shrugged his shoulders. There was nothing more he could say about the fight, but that still left them with a problem. "Perrelli is, or was, our leading radarman. We sail tomorrow. Do you want me to see if I can scrounge up a first-class from another ship?"

"Fat chance you'd have at this time of night," Slattery observed. He yawned and scratched his crotch. "We can get along without him." He handed Harry a message flimsy. "Here—look at this instruction from Pickle Head." The squadron's sobriquet for the Task Force Commander had its origin in the latter's appearance as he routinely inspected them at sea from the lofty height of *Argonne*'s bridge. The remarkably pointed skull, the bulging eyes, and his grayish-green complexion at sea created an effect not unlike that of the end of a large dill pickle peeking over the rim of a barrel. However, there was never any confusion about his instructions, and this message made its point very clearly: all vessels in the task force were to conserve fuel whenever possible in order to eliminate unnecessary refueling. The one exception to this standing order was when destroyers were changing station, or were assigned plane-guard duties. Then, commanding officers would be judged on how rapidly they could carry out their orders.

"We'll miss Perrelli all the more, then," Harry observed. "He was a past master at laying out a fast plot and sending maneuvering instructions to the bridge."

"When I was in the war, Red Lead, officers did that sort of thing themselves with a grease pencil on the back of an old envelope."

Harry risked a mild rejoinder: "Is that what finally drove the U-boats under?"

Slattery chuckled. "Might of at that. I always figured they went down to get out of the wind and snow. Even if it smelled of rancid oil and sauerkraut down there, at least it was warm—more than you could say for the rest of us."

"You were on the Murmansk run, weren't you?"

"Dorniers, U-boats, and an occasional Kraut cruiser all the way up. Four out of ten ships never made it; the rest of us just sweated all the way up. Never be another one like it, you better believe it. A man in the water lasted less than four minutes. I broke the record." Slattery pulled down the left shoulder of his grimy T-shirt, disclosing a large, freckled scar. "Tracer knocked me right off the bridge. The Dornier that got me got the ammunition ship behind us. She went up in one big *whoosh*. Blew a goddamned Carley float right into me. I just had strength to pull myself aboard. Came to in Russia with the best-looking nurse you ever saw. Russian winter's a good time and place to hole up, Red Lead. Good vodka and good women."

Harry shifted uneasily on his feet and glanced at his watch. He had a date with Diane, and Slattery in an expansive mood could go on for hours. "If you don't need me further, Captain, I've just time to catch the liberty boat. What do you want me to do about Dieter?"

"Leave him to me. And put a note in that famous daily notice of yours that any officer taking more than a minute to go a thousand yards changing station can count on loss of a day's liberty every time it happens."

"Captain, that means maneuvering at speeds above thirty knots—maybe at night and during periods of electronic silence. That's dangerous."

"Go screw your WAVE, Red Lead. I'm running this ship."

"He must be mad, Diane. Can you imagine those kids of ours, fresh out of school, ordering the ship about at high speed in the dark without a first-class radarman to help them? Christ, I'll have to be on the bridge all night, every night. You can't trust him."

"Harry, he knows what he's doing. He commanded long before you came aboard, you know."

"That may be true, but I'm going to sleep with my life jacket on in any case."

"Just so you come back to me."

The orchestra at the officers' club launched into a medley of old-timers. She squeezed his hand. "That's 'Diane' they're playing," she prompted.

Holding her in his arms on the dance floor, he began to unwind and forget his worries. She's good for me, he thought. She takes me out of myself. Maybe I'm just trying too hard.

When they returned to the table, she asked, "Where does the ship go tomorrow, Harry?"

He touched his *pousse-café* to hers. "I thought you Operations types knew all about those things. Or is this a test? Slip of the lip will sink a ship, that sort of thing."

"Oh, we know you're scheduled for a week of anti-submarine practice, but where you go is up to the Task Force Commander." Multicolored lights now began to sweep across the darkened room, sporadically illuminating them in the full spectrum of the electric palette.

"South to the Gulf Stream, probably. Then back to Block Island to turn and go out beyond the shipping lanes. It certainly won't be as much fun as it is here tonight."

She looked down at her plate. "Then why do you do it?"

"Huh?"

"I simply asked you what's so great about the sea that makes you keep coming back for more? I mean, suppose you got out? Suppose we *both* got out?"

"Diane," he laughed. "It's the only life I know."

"You could try another one."

"An office, paper work, petty little conspiracies to advance yourself—I'd be no good at that. Besides . . ."

"Yes?"

"Well, hard to say, but there are those moments. Like when you haul out of a bent-line screen at forty miles an hour, heeled over fifty degrees, the old rustbucket shivering and thumping under you, spray over the bow, flags straight out in the wind. I mean, you can put your hand on the bridge coaming and feel that ship talk to you."

"This ship and I are one," she said. "Melville."

"That's it. Then too, there's the duty, country bit. I'm like Collingwood, I guess."

"Collingwood?"

"Nelson's second in command. Whenever he was ashore, he liked to stroll the English countryside planting acorns. Each acorn the beginning of another English spar."

"Poor Mrs. Collingwood," she observed sadly.

Laughing, he threw up his hands. "Hey, time, please! I want to make love to a beautiful girl, not discuss life styles. Come on, let's dance."

Later, giddy and relaxed, they ended up in her room. He discovered *Tannhäuser* among her tapes, and they curled up on the sofa together to listen.

"I was silly to suggest giving up the Navy, wasn't I?" she whispered. The gentlest touch of his fingers explored the silken softness of her lower belly.

"Nothing about you is silly," he murmured into her ear. She took his hand and lifted it to her breasts.

"I guess I care too much about the men I love."

"I like you to care. I like you to love," he replied shushing her with a kiss.

She pulled him to her fiercely. "Harry, love me tonight. Stay with me."

"Until the dawn," he promised. "I'll catch the last boat back." He captured her hand and drew it down.

Her eyes widened, and he lifted her dress and slowly pressed his body to her in a gentle thrusting motion in time to the music. She shuddered each time he touched the moist softness of her. But then, gently, she disengaged herself. "Before this goes further, there are things that must be done."

While he waited he undressed, flinging his uniform into a battered chair. He winked at the sly face in the Hogarth, and out in the bay the red truck lights of *Somerset* winked back at him. He fingered the scar across the bridge of his nose and studied his own battered prizefighter's body, wishing suddenly that he were better-looking. A moment later, she called his name softly.

Unlike their hasty, fierce lovemaking of the afternoon before, this was a languorous affair. Later next morning he was to be astonished by her ability to evoke fresh passions when it seemed as though they would be impossible to attain. But this initial coupling was a long-drawn-out sensation of fingernails drawn across taut flesh, uninhibited experimentation, and sudden heights of throbbing emotion. At last, with a small cry, she spread herself before him and, arching her body, received him until he released them both with one final shuddering thrust of swollen flesh.

A millennium later, he lit a cigarette and sat up in bed. He caressed the back of her neck, smoothing down the little curls of moist hair. A blast of air rattled the window, and she drew herself closer to him. He looked down and was surprised to discover that she was already dozing lightly, her face composed and looking much like what she must have looked like as a little girl. There was an aura of innocence about her that made him regret his earlier suspicions. Finally he stubbed out his cigarette and curled up alongside her, resting easily in the warm cove of her flesh.

Quickly Dieter opened the padlock and slipped into the small compartment labeled AFTER STEERING. He switched on his flashlight, directing the beam to where the black, oiled cables controlling the destroyer's rudder pierced the after bulkhead. Deserted except during Captain's monthly inspection, the compartment housed a small steering wheel with a mechanical linkage to those same cables, the apparatus serving as a backup system in case of a hit on the bridge. His skull pounding beneath the bandages, Dieter remained undecided for a moment. Then, because of a wide frame that partially obscured that wire, he chose the starboard cable.

On his stomach now, he snaked alongside the wire and patiently wiped away the grease and rust that had collected beneath it. He was soon sweating and filthy for his efforts. Finally he was ready. He secured the thermite bomb directly under the cable with long ribbons of masking tape that completely covered the grenade except for the ugly head and safety pin. Beneath the curved arm of the detonator he gently bound two wired dynamite caps into place. Finally he crammed the batteries and clock into the remainder of the small space and taped them firmly into place. The clock was wound and running. He consulted the slip of paper given him by Willie and read again the cryptic message: *2330*. He set the alarm at eleven-thirty but did not pull out the stem. And he left the safety pin in the grenade. At last, still on his back, he squirmed from beneath the cable. He was sweating like a messcook and slippery as a greased snake, but the next job would be much easier. He had only to half-sever one small wire in the scanning radar.

The door swung open to the limit of the chain lock, and he rammed a foot into the narrow slit.

"Let me in, May," he growled. "I've money—*plenty* of money."

"No," she whispered forcefully. "Go away. We don't want your kind here."

"Let me in," he roared. "I'll call the police."

"Quiet, you fool." Alarm registered in her expression

as she saw him draw back as if to batter down the door. She gave in. "All right. You can come in for one drink."

"Drink," he sneered, once inside. He pulled out an enormous role of bills. "I've another appetite in mind."

From behind greasy, dyed red hair, May's eyes glittered greedily at the sight of the bills. "You rob a bank, or something?"

"Buy the girls some champagne. I won't be back for a long time." He stuffed a one-hundred-dollar bill down the front of May's wrapper. "I'll want the usual tonight."

"They don't like your idea of fun."

"Two hundred dollars each for ten minutes, nobody hurt, and no one the wiser. Don't make me laugh! I'll be upstairs. Two girls, and I don't mean two of those old bags you stable around here. Hurry—the boat's waiting."

Once upstairs, he turned into a small bedroom of peeling, fly-specked wallpaper. The naked bulb dangling from the frayed electric cord illuminated an unmade bed, the filthy sheets rumpled back to reveal gray tufts of mattress ticking. A Woolworth night table was the only other piece of furniture in the room. He stripped to his shorts and pulled a bottle of cheap whiskey from his overnight bag. Between great fiery gulps of liquor he waited, his breath coming in quick, nervous bursts.

"I'm Maria—in case you don't remember," said the short, fat, ugly girl in a cold, expressionless voice. She wore white-enameled high-heeled boots with pipe-clayed lacings and little brass ornaments. "This is Eileen." She indicated her partner, a young brunette with startled brown eyes, edged with fear. "May said two hundred each and one hundred for the house."

"You'll do." He grunted and peeled off five one-hundred-dollar bills, which he threw on the table. "On the bed," he growled at the younger girl. Although her eyes had lit up at the sight of the cash, she was still reluctant.

"May—May said it wouldn't hurt."

"On the mattress," he said roughly. He stepped out of his shorts and from the bag produced four silken cords, with which he proceeded to bind the young girl spread-eagled across the mattress. When he had finished, her ribs showed plainly, and her small breasts flattened against her chest. "Two fried eggs on an ironing board," he snarled. "Whatta'ya so careful about?"

His breath came in short, eager bursts now as he dipped once again into the bag. When she saw the small whip with its three short lashes of thick silk cord, she lost her nerve.

"I've changed my mind. It'll hurt."

He ignored her. "You know what to do?" he asked Maria.

"Never had any complaints before."

He sat on the edge of the mattress and ran his hands lightly over the young body. He moaned softly, spittle forming at the corner of his sensuous lips. Maria sat behind him, her fingers exploring his crotch. At last she seized his testicles and began to squeeze gently. He groaned aloud and then lashed out with the whip. The young girl screamed, although the silken cord had left her unmarked as yet.

"Easy on her, Duke," Maria cautioned—but from the expression that had now come over Slattery's face, she doubted he had heard her.

Thirteen

Proceeding on a southerly heading, the small formation of ships had, by early evening of the following Monday, traversed sufficient parallels of latitude to be at the northern edge of the Gulf Stream's zone of influence. Once there, the climate changed markedly. A softness crept into the air. The seas calmed, changing from slate gray to a sparkling turquoise. The shrieking gulls that had followed them out to sea deserted the fantail, replaced by an occasional porpoise that surfaced to gambol about the rolling, hissing knife-edge that was the destroyer's stem.

Oblivious to more prolonged seasonal transitions, the crew reacted quickly to this change in environment. Foul-weather gear and scowls disappeared, replaced by shirt sleeves and smiles. New ambition seized both officers and men; in a twinkling, paint pots appeared. Red chromate disappeared under slate gray, brasswork glistened in the warming rays of the sun, and canvas was scrubbed white again. This premature taste of summer was enough to set aflame even the dourest of the New Englanders who composed most of *Somerset*'s crew. There was one exception.

Harry St. John could not seem to lift himself from the trough of a depression that had enveloped him the moment *Somerset* sailed. He felt tired and edgy. Despite the buoyant environment, his head ached, his tongue felt furry. He was coming down with something—just what he did not know, but he suspected it was more mental than physical. Even with his normal robust health, he could not enjoy this preview of summer, no matter how glorious the sea and weather, if he was to follow the Admiral's instructions to "suspect everyone, trust no one." He did not believe that he was in any physical danger. He preferred to believe that *Somerset*'s wardroom was exactly what it appeared to be: a baker's dozen of spirited young officers commanded by a somewhat eccentric leader. The dark shadow cast by Cutter's suspicion of a madman among his shipmates seemed to make Harry physically ill. Chapman must have sensed as much. Following eight o'clock reports on Tuesday, he took Harry aside.

"You look *terrible,*" he observed. "How do you feel?"

They were standing in the small passageway just off the pilothouse, and the red lighting used in that space to facilitate adaptation to night vision served to emphasize the greenish pallor of Harry's features.

"In a word, lousy. Maybe I'm working too hard." Drowsiness overcame Harry, and he tried unsuccessfully to stifle a yawn.

"You're just tired, that's all. Get a good night's sleep and you'll snap out of it."

"Can't, Chappie. Slattery asked me to take James's watch tonight."

"You sure you feel up to taking on the eight-to-twelve? I ain't stood a deck watch in years, but I'll be glad to try, if you promise to get some sleep."

"Thanks, Chappie, but I think I can handle it. We'll need you in the engine room tonight. If the carrier launches, we may have to go to plane-guard station."

"Oh, is there a launch scheduled for tonight?" Chapman looked bemused. "Wonder why Slattery didn't mention it to me. Well, no matter—I'll be down there tonight anyway."

I'm going to have to shape up, Harry thought. He was so tired that he couldn't even remember the schedule of events listed in the Operations Order.

"Appreciate your offer, Chappie. I'll give you as much notice as I can if we do have to change station."

"Just remember, it's no disgrace to be sick—even seasick," Chapman remonstrated in parting.

The small space in the narrow passageway freed by his departure was filled almost immediately.

"Mr. St. John? Chief Nielson here."

"Right, Chief. What's on your mind?"

"Two things, Commander. First, Dieter asked me if it was okay to swing out the launch tonight."

"What the hell for? I thought I had put him on report." Harry found himself irritated at the very mention of Dieter's name.

"Dieter wants to finish the job he started on Block Island."

"At night?"

"He says he'll rig a light and use a life jacket with a safety line, and the bowhookman will act as a line tender. He works at night like that often."

Harry rebelled against the thought that anyone should have to do routine ship's upkeep at night, but with the elaborate safety precautions planned, it was probably safe enough. Dieter might even be performing some sort of self-inflicted penance to atone for his two recent scrapes. And it was generally bad policy to discourage any man from putting in unrequested overtime. Finally, Dieter was Slattery's pet. The last thing Harry wanted in the next few hours was a fight with his Commanding Officer.

"Okay," he agreed reluctantly. "What else?"

"My transfer, sir. Have you seen or heard anything about

my request?" There was a touch of desperation in Nielson's voice. Harry glanced up sharply and tried unsuccessfully to read the Chief's expression in the gloom.

"You'll have to ask Slattery about it. I didn't even know you had put in for transfer."

Nielson turned away, deep disappointment evident in his manner.

"Anything *I* can do, Chief?"

"Speaking frankly, yes, sir. That was my third request for transfer ashore. My wife's been very sick lately. I was hoping that with you aboard . . ."

Damn, thought Harry in vexation. Nothing but problems on the ship tonight. And tonight was not the time for Harry to attempt a solution to the family problems of the destroyer's leading enlisted man.

"I'll have a talk with the Skipper tomorrow, Chief. I'll see what I can do, but I'm not promising anything."

He left Nielson there and eased into the pilothouse. From somewhere in the darkness Slattery loomed beside him and thrust a mug of hot coffee into his hand.

"Drink that, Number One. It'll put lead in your pencil, you better believe it! If you need me, I'll be watching the movie in the wardroom."

Gratefully, Harry sipped the scalding fluid. The instant the coffee went down, it seemed to give him renewed strength. Tolley switched on the small lamp over the chart table—the sudden glare blinding to Harry's eyes, which were already adjusted to night vision.

"Here's the Night Order Book, Commander. The Skipper just finished writing tonight's chapter and verse."

Tolley made room for Harry at the table. Once Harry understood the instructions and initialed the book, the responsibility for the maneuvering of the ship would transfer officially to him. Tolley would then be released from further deck duties until his next watch.

In contrast to his otherwise disorderly habits, Slattery's

hand was surprisingly fine and precise. His writing slanted to the left and was clearly scribed in ball-point. The thrust of Slattery's message was clear enough—instructions that any conscientious commanding officer might have laid down.

> Steaming in company with *Argonne* (Lord) and *Pickering* (Barney) on course 045° true, at speed 15 knots. Latitude is 41° N, longitude 71.7° W. *Argonne* is on a line of bearing 315° relative, distant 3,000 yards. Boilers #1 and #2 are on the line. Power is supplied by ship's service generator #2. No exercises are expected for tonight. Ship's coxswain has permission to swing out the whaleboat and carry out necessary repairs. Call me if any signals are put in the air. Call me if any radar contacts are plotted to pass within 5 miles of *Somerset*. Call me for any signals that *Argonne* may make, or any incidents that justify attention. Remember, I would rather be called a thousand times unnecessarily than not called once when I should have been notified.
>
> Slattery, CDR, USNR

"Looks easy enough tonight, Paul. Let me just check your position." Harry doubled over the radar repeater and tracked the range pip through *Argonne*. The bearing was exactly zero-zero-one. The range was twenty-nine hundred and fifty yards.

"I've been using ten turns under fifteen knots, Commander. She drifts back slowly, but one-five-zero RPM's pulls you away fast."

"Thanks, Paul. I'll give it a try when we make up the fifty yards and one degree."

He returned to the Night Order Book, carefully drew a line through the name JAMES, printed in his own name, and then put his initials beside it. He slipped the book into his back pocket.

"I have the conn," he announced to the pilothouse crew. "Add ten turns!"

"One-five-zero revolutions, sir," announced the lee helmsman when the engine-room telegraph answered.

The faint sound of a roaring lion issued from the wardroom below. "Movie's starting, Commander. She's all yours." Tolley flipped a carefree salute in Harry's direction and disappeared down the weather-deck ladder on the run.

A faint mist was falling when Harry stepped outside to make a visual check of the horizon. Overhead, clouds rushed past like enormous low-flying airships, occasionally revealing cold white stars a millennium away. An acrid taste of soot from the number-one funnel poisoned the atmosphere, and the smell of stack gas lay heavy upon the destroyer's upperworks. The seas were calm and flashed fluorescence as the thrusting bows of the vessel bisected the semicircle of his vision. Harry tried unsuccessfully to shake off a feeling of foreboding, as though the vessel with all aboard were rushing to some private hell.

To rid himself of this bleak outlook, he turned his thoughts to the happiest event of his most recent days. He wondered what decision Diane would come to with regard to the two of them. She, with her pick of several hundred handsome officers who shared her more glamorous world of Newport shore duty, could hardly be expected to be interested in a somewhat battered run-of-the-mill destroyer officer. And yet, she *was* interested. To ward off the blackness of the night, he cloaked himself in that flattering thought and began to nod dreamily. Moments later, he had to stop himself from falling completely asleep.

Harry couldn't recall ever having felt more exhausted. In fact, the drugging effect of the stack gas and his own nausea seemed to preclude all but the most minor mental effort. Like a heavyweight boxer rising to the count of nine, Harry felt his legs wobbly; his stomach, a knot of aches. The stimulating effect of Slattery's coffee had by now been overridden by a feeling of anesthesia that seemed to spread to every part of his body. Almost unable to focus his mind, he was thankful that this was to be an uneventful watch. But was it?

Vaguely he knew that he had best check the Operations Order to make certain that the watch was to be a rest period between the exercises. By sheer willpower, he did manage to stagger to the chart table, where a small rack of reference materials was kept on an overhead shelf.

The Operations Order was not there. Damn, he thought. The books seemed to swim crazily before him. He fumbled several times through the shelf before giving up the search. Perhaps Perrelli had the Operations Plan down in the Combat Information Center. He thumbed up the *CIC* button on the bridge speaker and asked for the radarman.

"Sorry, Bridge," came the reply; "Perrelli's ashore in the hospital."

"Has anyone down there seen the Operations Order?"

"Bridge, we haven't even had time to look for it. There's something wrong with the radar. We been trying to repair it. I was just going to call and ask permission to close down the radar to see if we can fix it."

"How long will that take?"

"Ten minutes if Perrelli was here. Now I don't know."

Through the fog in his mind, Harry numbly reasoned that in this simple station-keeping situation he could probably get along without radar ranges for perhaps an hour or so. If necessary, he could always call *Argonne* and request a reading of the distance between them. Indeed, if he got very far off station, *Argonne* would call him.

"Give me one last range to the carrier and then go ahead and shut down when you're ready."

"I'm getting exactly three thousand yards, Bridge."

"Okay, go ahead and secure down there." He released the button and turned back to the lee helmsman.

"Drop ten turns," he mumbled.

If Tolley was right, this would hold the old destroyer on station for a while. Aware of the impression he had made on the pilothouse crew, he returned clumsily to the port bridge wing. There, his elbows locked tightly over the coaming, he fought sleep as long as he could. Leaning on the bridge structure in this manner, he finally dozed off.

After what could have been either a moment or an eternity, he became conscious of a soft modulation in the background noise emitting from the speaker of the primary tactical radio circuit. Someone aboard *Argonne* was pressing the key prior to transmitting. He pulled himself together and tried to regain full awareness. He glanced at his watch; he had been on the destroyer's bridge for three hours.

Then the radio blasted forth. "Dandy, this is Lord. Fox, Corpen, one-seven-zero. Take plane-guard station!"

The carrier was going to launch aircraft, and *Somerset* was to circle and come up astern of *Argonne*. As though moving in a dream, Harry found himself in the pilothouse. He groped for the right solution to the simple tactical problem. He knew that for a safe maneuver, the destroyer would have to turn outside the carrier's path.

"Left full rudder, full speed ahead," he finally ordered. Staggering to the sound-powered phones, he punched viciously every one of the buttons. Voices, muffled and indistinct, came on the line from all corners of the ship. He waited until he heard the one voice he wanted to hear.

Slattery growled, "What the hell's going on?"

"Sick . . . Captain . . ." It was all he could say. He dropped the phone, fell out on the bridge wing, and vomited.

He lay out on the bridge for what seemed an eternity. Then rough hands seized him. Voices blurred in the background. A rapid series of helm and engine orders concluded with a last chilling command: "All back emergency, left hard rudder!"

Something cool and damp caressed his face, washing away the vile ejection of his outraged stomach. An odor of cheap whiskey assailed his nostrils.

"On your feet, you drunken bastard," shouted Slattery, roughly hauling him upright and slamming him against the coaming. "I want you to see what *you've* done." Slattery left him there and dived for the collision-alarm handle. The alarm went off with a mind-shattering whooping, which was answered almost immediately by a similar alarm from almost directly overhead. Harry raised his eyes.

Looming over the destroyer, the enormous bulk of *Argonne* plunged down upon them. Under the overhang of the huge flight deck, the dark Atlantic roiled upward in a frothing gray turbulence. In the comparative stillness following the last *whoop-whoop* of the collision alarm, he heard distinctly the throbbing of *Argonne*'s enormous turbines. The red, white, and green running lights of the aircraft carrier bathed the destroyer's pilothouse in a bizarre colored brightness. *Somerset*'s bridge watch seemed frozen at their stations. At last, the helmsman looked up with an expression of sudden curiosity. He spun the wheel several times in both directions and with an expression of disbelief said, "Steering control is lost and the helm doesn't respond, sir."

On *Argonne*'s bridge, an officer discarded his night glasses and stabbed a forefinger in *Somerset*'s direction, shouting something that was lost in the wind. For a brief instant, Harry thought *Somerset* would somehow slide out from under the carrier's bows. But then *Argonne* rose even higher above them, the cruel knife edge of the bows pointed directly between the destroyer's funnels. The clock ticked over to 2330. Then *Argonne* struck.

Fourteen

Argonne, almost twenty-five times the size of *Somerset,* tore through the little destroyer with extraordinary ease. So little resistance was offered by the destroyer, in fact, that on the carrier's bridge, from where the broad expanse of the flight deck blocked a view of what was happening seventy feet below, *Argonne*'s crew members first thought the destroyer might even have escaped safely. A small tremor passed through the carrier. Otherwise, from *Argonne*'s vantage point, there was no immediate evidence of collision.

Aboard the destroyer, however, calamity struck. *Argonne*'s bow penetrated *Somerset* just aft of the number-two funnel. The destroyer heeled sharply to port and collapsed at the point of impact with a shriek of tortured metal. The keel, which might just have held the vessel together if it had been forced downward, was instead lifted out of the water and rolled upward towards the cruel blade of *Argonne*'s bow. A fraction of a second after the destroyer's hull yielded to the impact, the keel snapped apart. The two halves of the mortally wounded vessel were flung aside, their shattered ends acting as mouths to the onrushing seas. Open electrical lines showered sparks as they shorted out on contact with the Atlantic Ocean. Her fuel tanks burst, the destroyer's halves commenced sinking in spreading pools of her own oil. The stern section, with open hatches for ventilation to the crew's compartment, went down in forty-five seconds. The bow stayed upright only seconds longer, a large air bubble forming just aft of the chain locker, until the enormous pressure caused by the flooding sea blew out the deck plating.

Most of the crew died moments after being jolted awake. A few of those already awake at the moment of impact managed to get off the ship in time to save themselves. Two hundred did not.

Belowdecks, Charlie Chapman died quickly. His mind, occupied with the maddening paper work involved in accounting for *Somerset*'s fuel allowance and constant machinery overhauls, barely detected the frantic ringing of the engine bells. He glanced up in sudden irritation at the cacaphonic signal for "All back emergency," and then, noting the expression of terror on the engineer's face, arose from his small desk and strode over to the throttles.

A hiss became a roar as the bypass valve was opened and superheated steam, direct from the headers, rushed full into the backing turbine. *Somerset*'s racing shafts tore up two bearings before they ground to a halt. Then, in a cloud of steam and with an enormous clatter and spray of oil from the mutilated bearings, the shafts began rotating in the opposite direction.

The throttleman nervously wiped his sweating hands on a hank of oily cotton waste. He lifted an eyebrow in silent inquiry. Chappie nodded and walked back to the sound-powered phone that connected to the bridge. The Chief Engineer turned and faced starboard as he punched the buzzer. Then the collision alarm went off, and the tense engine-room gang, already alerted by the backing bell, sprinted from all corners of the compartment toward the escape ladder.

Chappie first felt the vessel roll over. Next, the deck gratings rose under him until he had to grasp the telephone jackbox to keep from falling. Before his horrified eyes, the starboard side of the ship split apart as *Argonne*'s bow pierced his engine room. The men who had managed to make it partway up the ladder fell immediately upon their shipmates below. Three electrical cables snapped before the main steam line let go. The steam line bent to port. It blew out through the expansion joint directly facing Chapman. A jet of superheated steam, one half inch thick and over eleven hundred degrees in temperature, so hot that it was invisible to the naked eye, cut Chapman's torso in half at the waist and launched the blackened halves backward in the direction of the bilges.

Jack Poindexter never even knew that a collision had occurred. Sandwiched between the coarse, explosive laughter of Slattery and the snores of a dozing Dennis Ramsey, he had suffered through the second reel of the officers' movie with a nagging New England conscience. The movie was a thunderingly bad Western with a low-budget cast and a script seemingly concocted as the shooting took place. It concerned the affairs of a gun-fighting priest and had been produced in Italy for wide-screen presentation and stereophonic sound track. The print was on its sixth tour through the Atlantic Fleet, and considerably the worse for wear. Now, with the picture projected against the wardroom tablecloth by an untrained operator and with the sound track fed through a single battered speaker, the result was disaster. During the break between the second and third reels, Poindexter gave it up and fled to the sanctuary of the Supply Office.

Seated at his own desk in the peace and quiet of his own

domain, he felt his spirits pick up rapidly. He detested sea duty with a passion highly uncharacteristic of him, and he hated *Somerset* more than any assignment that he might have drawn. However, his assignment to the destroyer had been of his own choosing.

Graduating from Supply Officer School with romantic notions of the life at sea, he had turned down any number of assignments more suited to his temperament and had asked for an assignment with the destroyer forces. The very moment he had stepped aboard *Somerset* and encountered Duke Slattery for the first time, he knew that it had been the worst mistake of his life. Now he had only another twenty-three days until his transfer ashore, an event expected to be the Renaissance of his career to date.

As he contemplated that singularly pleasant event, even the problem of the destroyer's enormous cash supply ceased to disturb him. Pleased with his upcoming good fortune, he checked over the payroll list for the second time that day. The destroyer lurched into a high-speed maneuver, and he recalled another good reason for his elation at being transferred ashore: it was almost impossible to do accurate accounting when one was being thrown about as though he were aboard a giant roller coaster. He finished totaling his accounts and opened the safe to put the cash needed for tomorrow's payday into a separate bag, so as to avoid confusion when actual disbursement began the next morning. The destroyer righted herself and began vibrating like a huge tuning fork. He had long ago lost interest in the activities of those fools up on the bridge. He was simply grateful that the ship was back on an even keel. He swung open the heavy Mosler door. An instant later, just as he was whistling a snatch from "Hello, Dolly!" the collision alarm went off. He looked up in vexation.

Jack Poindexter barely had time to recognize the blade end of the supply-room fire axe as it descended upon him, though not time enough to recognize the wielder. The cruel weapon neatly split his features in two and drove him backward over his chair and into the yawning safe. Had his vision not been so impaired, he would have seen the O-1 deck buckle above him, and the starboard anchor of *Argonne* neatly remove the number-two funnel cap.

Chief Lars Nielson didn't even get damp that night. His discussion with St. John had left unresolved the question of exactly where he stood with regard to his transfer, and he felt reluctant to let the matter drop. On the other hand, the only officer who had ever displayed enough gumption to take on Slattery was Harry St. John, and he was now on watch and unavailable.

Nielson, unwilling to give up and go below, prowled the main deck. Solitude was hard to come by on that particular night. Despite the faint mist, it seemed as though most of the crew were on the main deck.

About ten o'clock, things quieted down. The crew's movie ended, and small groups of sailors made their way below to their bunks. Nielson remained in the shadows. He lit a cigar and pondered the bitter pill of another year before he could exercise his option to retire. Sometime after eleven he finished the cigar. By then he was finally ready to turn in. Then a burst of excited voices on one of the destroyer's radio speakers caught his ear. He glanced upward at the bridge. Something was wrong. The radar antenna was locked into place. The vessel was heeling into a sharp turn.

He went up the weather-deck ladder two rungs at a time, reaching the top just as the collision alarm went off. Stunned by the unexpected sound, he stopped short beside the flag bag. Before his startled eyes the ship's Executive Officer stumbled into a corner of the bridge wing, apparently passing-out drunk and weaving on his feet. The odor of vomit and sour whiskey rankled Nielson's nostrils. He glanced to the right, and the expression on his face turned to horror.

To Nielson, *Argonne*'s path through the destroyer was mostly a series of violent crunches, as though the destroyer had run aground. He went over to port as the vessel rolled sharply. His flailing arms, desperate for any support, grasped a thin wire cable. To his utter astonishment, in that next instant Lars Nielson found himself flying through the air while dangling forty feet over the sea. *Somerset* had disappeared beneath him.

It would take some time before Nielson could believe that he had been fantastically lucky that night. The Chief dangled on the end of a guy wire that supported one of *Argonne*'s radio antennae. The wire was used to pull out and support the long yagi antenna, which, happily for Nielson, was not now in use. He was flying through the air as though he were a circus aerialist, his trapeze being attached to the aircraft carrier.

The small guy wire cut deep into his palms. Nielson worked slowly inboard along the wire, as much to ease the excruciating pain in his palms as to follow his own blind instinct for survival. Just as he decided that he could no longer stand the pain and must drop into that vast black void beneath him, a dazzling burst of light illuminated him. *Argonne* was turning on every light aboard to provide a beacon for *Somerset*'s men in the sea. Nielson found himself the target of a cluster of searchlights. *Argonne*'s sailors raced to his aid with cheers of encouragement. With a final burst of desperate energy, Nielson went hand over bleeding hand toward safety.

Paul Tolley stepped out of the wardroom and directly into the Atlantic. The main deck was already underwater. The wardroom followed seconds later. The stern end of the destroyer, now distant some one hundred yards, was already going down. A great crackle of sparks from a whipping electrical cable illuminated the area momentarily. With horror, Tolley saw the unfamiliar propellers and dripping rudder rise to the vertical. Then the stern section plunged bottomward in a vast cloud of steam and with a curious hollow moan, as though the vessel herself were crying out in despair.

Tolley clawed his way through a two-inch-thick oil sludge that now lay on the surface of the sea. He struck out hurriedly, for he was afraid the depth charges carried on the stern section might explode. As he struggled into a temporarily oil-free area, he turned and watched the bow upend. Once at the perpendicular, the destroyer's forward half floated somewhat longer than had the stern. Then the deck plating burst, spilling out a vast catenary of anchor chain, and the bow went down with a rush, almost engulfing Tolley in a wave of water and oil. He was too startled to grasp the full significance of what had happened until, with the last of the crunching sounds and as the last large bubble burst from the depths, an eerie silence settled upon him.

Tolley was a strong swimmer. He rolled over on his back and raised his head as far out of the oily sea as was possible. No other survivors appeared within the circle of his vision, and there appeared to be nothing in the way of debris to which he might cling. He kept scissoring himself away from the center of the slick, but it was tough going. The oil was spreading as fast as he could swim or faster. And keeping afloat in a sea with three-foot swells was very different from bathing along the shore.

Once, from very far away, he thought he heard the sound of a motor whaleboat, but then the sound faded and there were only black night, sea, and oil. He thought wildly for a moment about sharks, and that grim thought inspired him to kick harder. Oil now lay like a black hand over his features. He could no longer open his eyes. Oil burned his nostrils, clogged his ears, and seared his guts. He kept kicking. Vaguely he became aware of a deep throbbing pain in his left ankle. He kept on kicking.

An eternity later, just when he thought that he could no longer go on, the sound of a whaleboat engine reached him. The sputter of the diesel was soon accompanied by the musical burble of water breaking against the small boat's stem. He tried unsuccessfully to open his burning eyes. He was temporarily blind. He tried to shout but only an unrecognizable croak came forth. Feebly he waved an arm.

A boathook appeared over his now unrecognizable face and twisted itself into the fabric of his shirt. The words "Here's *one,* anyway" floated out of the night. Strong arms hoisted him over the gunwale as Tolley finally fainted from shock and exhaustion.

Harry St. John rose to his feet quickly, almost flattening Chief Nielson in the process. An instant later he was knocked sprawling again, this time the sky above him blotted out by *Argonne*'s enormous flight deck. He threw his arms over his face and jackknifed his body into a corner as *Argonne* rushed over them with the explosive force of a thundering locomotive. When he rolled over and looked back, Nielson had vanished. So had the after end of the destroyer, amputated just aft of where he lay. The pilothouse was deserted.

There was no sickness or tiredness now, only the instinct for survival. One look at *Somerset*'s remains and he knew there was nothing he could do for ship or crew. If he was going to save himself, he had better do so right away. Quickly he kicked off his shoes and slid into a life jacket. Taking a flashlight with him, he simply stepped off the bridge level, a platform which by this time was almost even with the sea. He was none too soon.

The bridge sank under him as the bow rose in the air. Pushed away by the wash and buoyed by the jacket, he was able to keep his head clear of the spreading oil. Holding the flashlight above him with one hand, he sidestroked away from the destroyer's grave. He swam methodically, not even turning around when *Somerset*'s bow section plunged bottomward.

Unlike Tolley, who had gone off the other side of the destroyer, Harry swam through an ample supply of flotsam. Only a few minutes after he had gone into the water, his flailing arm encountered a bobbing object riding low on the oil slick. He scrambled out of the water and switched on the flash.

He was lying atop one of the destroyer's large wooden deck gratings. He rotated the flash over his head several times and shouted to attract attention. He swept the area around him with the beam of light, but could see only debris on the sea. As *Argonne* turned, he thought he saw the destroyer's whaleboat disappear into the darkness, running full speed for the carrier. He shouted again several times, but his only reply was silence. Like a nightmare being rerun, memories of *Yellowbird*'s last moments burst through the barriers he had long ago erected in his mind. Then, quite suddenly, he lost control of himself. Tears of sorrow coursed down his oil-blackened cheeks. How many men this time? he wondered. Twice in his life he had lost his shipmates in this violent manner. The thought occurred to him that he was in fact a Jonah. He found himself mumbling aloud, the words a prayer from his midshipman upbringing.

"Almighty Father, whose way is in the sea, whose path is in the great waters, whose command is over all and whose love never faileth . . . Help me so to live that I can stand unashamed and unafraid before my shipmates . . . And if I should miss the mark, give me courage to try again . . ."

Give me courage to try again. He had tried again. God, how he had tried. Now he was finished. He should have gone down with the ship. When one of *Argonne*'s boats finally hove into view, he felt himself unworthy of rescue. He wanted to drift with the rest of the wreckage, to remain in the cold sea with the shipmates he had just killed. But they found him and they took him aboard, the man who had sunk his ship, the outcast of the black waters.

Fifteen

"What did he say?"

Dieter carefully replaced the watertight seals over the transmitter/receiver capsules before replying. "You are to be picked up two nights from today. I am to return to the mainland and await further instructions."

Rage blazed in Slattery's eyes. "Good God, man! Didn't he say anything about a doctor? Christ, smell my leg!"

"You will receive excellent medical treatment aboard the submarine." Dieter's voice was cold, expressionless. He suddenly snarled, "Bah! You Americans are soft. Without television, overheated houses, and those incredible amounts of food you waste, you are nothing." He snapped his fingers in the air. "If your leg bothers you, then as you say here, you must take up the notch in the belt."

Slattery recoiled helplessly in the face of this new evidence of the reversal of their positions. He shivered and tried a new tack. "Please, Dieter . . . Colonel Dieter . . . let me have another drink. It's the pain."

Dieter regarded him coldly. In the few areas where Slattery's great black beard didn't sprout, the man's skin was an unhealthy gray. His eyes, red-yellow with pain, were sunk into black pools. His leg was, of course, beyond saving, the jagged end of bone—what did they call it—tibia—projecting through greenish-yellow skin swollen with corruption. It was going to be touch and go to bring him off the island alive. "You need not fear, Commander Slattery. I have radioed the submarine that your leg is broken and you require urgent medical assistance. I will see you safely aboard. It will be a short but painful journey, I think." He proffered the almost-empty flask of whiskey. "I advise you not to drink it all. There are forty-eight more hours."

Duke Slattery clutched at the small silver flask and sucked greedily. He moaned softly. "Oh, God, but that's good." He recapped the flask and lay back on the cold, wet sand. "None of this would have happened if you had used a little care with Abel," he suddenly whined. "Ten days without heat on this fucking island. My God, smell my leg. I've lost it for sure!"

"May I make two observations, my dear Slattery? With respect to your leg, if you had dived over the side an instant after I had freed the launch, you wouldn't have come down into the boat like a great, thrashing black bear. Instead, I would have fished you from the water according to our plan. With respect to Abel, how was I to know that he had not only found the missing rotors where you had hidden them, but pocketed one as well?"

"You might have searched him before you pushed him over the side."

"Fool, I told you he fought like a tiger. You were supposed to have drugged him. It was all I could do to throw him into the propellers. It was just bad luck that trawler happened to snag the body."

Slattery saw the choler rise in Dieter's face. Dieter aroused was unpredictable. Slattery tried to change the subject.

"Can't we have a bigger fire, Colonel?" he pleaded, fishing from his pocket a small twist of paper to help spread the flames.

"And alert everyone on this cursed island of yours? Again, I seem to recall that it was you who selected this cove. You were the one who left the kerosene heater aboard the day we unloaded our equipment here." Dieter sneered. "After a taste of our Siberian winter, you may come to regard this island as a Finnish sauna."

"Is that where I'm going—Siberia?"

"I have no idea, Comrade Slattery. Your work here is finished. You will be debriefed in that same little house on Gorki Street where we first met so many years ago. Useful work will be found for you. If you had been able to dispose of St. John it would have pleased me personally, but I also say I respect the decision. When the Americans finally begin to catch on, the entire operation explodes in front of them." Dieter snapped his fingers crisply in the cold, dry air. "There is even a fool left behind to take the blame. All that now remains is to rejoin our comrades and sink the launch. You may pursue your curious passions, no longer fearing release of that interesting film we once saw together."

"And the murder charge?"

"So long ago!" Dieter smiled. "I might even send over a good word from America."

"Your fingerprints will give you away."

"There are still comrades ashore to assist me."

Slattery shivered uncontrollably. He rose up on his elbows. "Why can't they take me off now? I'm of no further use to you."

"Because I haven't ordered it," Dieter snapped. "I have told headquarters that our position here is secure. We will wait for the snow."

Brutally, Dieter suddenly swung the walkie-talkie around

in a wide arc so that its long antenna raked the length of Slattery's injured leg. With a scream of excruciating pain, Slattery fell back upon the hard sand.

"You may well curse, Comrade," Dieter snarled. "Your screams will help keep you warm, and you have only the gulls to disturb. The few houses here on this side of the island are all deserted for the winter."

That afternoon, Pozo King took Harry aside as spectators and witnesses filed from the courtroom. He handed Harry several sheets of yellow rough-draft paper. "Hawk asked me to prepare this," he said with embarrassment. "I thought you might as well see it."

Hawk had filed three charges: culpable inefficiency in the performance of duty; conduct to the prejudice of good order and discipline; and finally (with an eye to taxpayer dollars), not using his best efforts to prevent the unlawful destruction of public property. Pozo had laid it all out, copying the legalese directly from *Courts and Boards*:

> In that Harry Lawrence St. John, now a Lieutenant Commander, USN, while so serving as Officer of the Deck on board USS *Somerset,* a steam vessel engaged in night maneuvers with other naval vessels of Task Force 94.1.2, on the evening of March 3rd, at Latitude 41 degrees North and Longitude 72 degrees West, did then and there fail to issue and to see effected such timely orders as were necessary to cause the said vessel, USS *Somerset,* to keep from the path of USS *Argonne,* as it was his duty to do, and by reason of such inefficiency, the said vessel, USS *Somerset,* collided at the time and place aforesaid with the said USS *Argonne,* as a result of which collision the said USS *Somerset* was sunk.

A fat bluebottle fly that had somehow survived the winter cold buzzed noisily against the windowpane. Pozo took a scrap of paper and fastidiously trapped the insect within it. "I don't understand," Harry said finally. "In the legal sense, what does culpable mean?"

"The dictionary definition, I think: deserving of blame or censure. In order to sustain a conviction under this charge, *Courts and Boards* specifies that it must be shown that the accused was actually in charge when the events occurred. Harry, you better get yourself a good lawyer."

"You mean if I can't prove that Slattery relieved me before the collision, I'm cooked?"

"Precisely."

"Do *you* think the court believes Slattery was there?"

Pozo slowly shook his head. "Not a chance, brother."

"Then I'm done for?"

With a snap of his fingers, Pozo made a small twist of the paper, crushing the bluebottle within it. "Like *that*," he said, tossing the paper into the wastebasket.

The next day, Hawk announced an unexpected reprieve from another day of testimony. The principal witnesses and the court members were taken aboard two new destroyer leaders, which immediately proceeded to the scene of the collision. The court hoped that the visit might jog the survivors' memories to reveal some new aspect of the disaster. The charges to be brought against Harry would send shock waves all through the fleet. The conviction must be airtight with no Dreyfus-like aftermath. For most of *Somerset*'s survivors, crowding the bridge and upperworks of one sleek vessel, it was a painful experience. The worst came at the end.

Before the ships turned for home, a simple rite took place. With heads bared to the cold afternoon breeze, *Somerset*'s remaining crew members assembled on the fantail. The DesLant chaplain spoke softly on the heaving afterdeck: "Eternal Father, strong to save . . ." A wreath was placed on the oil-streaked water, a volley fired in the air, and Taps sounded. Then the powerful vessels raced for home, their engines throbbing, their ensigns streaming flat out in the breeze. Harry, a leper among his own shipmates, brooded on the flag bridge.

Slattery . . . Slattery. He cursed the name. God, if there's a restless grave, let it be his. And himself, sick like that puppy James before him, powerless to prevent disaster. James had been the lucky one. Gloomily he watched the vessel's stem lance through the creaming foam, each pulse of the screw bring him closer to public humiliation and imprisonment. Sweet Mother of God, how could it happen? Fate had caught him up, like Ahab, and destroyed him.

Another destined for punishment was the destroyer's Operations Officer, Paul Tolley. The Lieutenant's youth and the obviously painful white cast on his leg evoked sympathy, but the other side of the ledger was weighted with two hundred lives. Hawk, sure of one, pressed for two victims. After discovering that Tolley had remained at the officers' movie during the last maneuver, Hawk probed deeper.

"Is it not standard procedure for the Combat Information Center to keep a plot of the ship's movements and to provide maneuvering recommendations to the bridge?"

"Yes, sir."

"And did your C.I.C. maintain such a plot?"

"Usually, yes, sir."

"Don't avoid the question, please. I'm not asking what you usually did, Lieutenant. I'm asking about *this* particular maneuver on the night of collision." Hawk stabbed a finger toward the blackboard.

"I already told you. Our radar went out and was not repaired by the time we started the turn. We were blind and useless to the bridge."

"Why did the radar go out?"

"We never discovered, sir. It may have been because we had an inexperienced man on the set."

"Who couldn't repair it, get it going?"

"Yes, sir."

"Where was your usual radarman?"

God, thought Harry, two hundred lives! All because Perrelli and Dieter chose to get in a fight.

"In the hospital, sir."

"I see," Hawk said dryly. "You had no training program which would have developed an equally skilled replacement?"

Tolley glanced apologetically at Harry, as if to say that now, when it was too late, he saw what Harry had been after. "No, sir," he confessed sadly.

"Could you not maintain a tactical plot of the maneuver on the dead-reckoning tracer—the D.R.T.?"

"It would have been possible. However, as you know, the D.R.T. is quite inaccurate compared with radar."

"Inaccurate?"

"Yes, sir. My guess is that it wouldn't have been worth the effort."

"I'm afraid your guess isn't good enough, Lieutenant," Hawk snapped. "You have just told us you had no training program to prepare a replacement for the only good radarman you had. You didn't bother to provide recommendations to the bridge through the use of a substitute plotting device. Your reason for not doing so, you tell us, is because after barely two years in the Navy, you have concluded that all of those expensive electronic units installed aboard all of those ships are 'not worth the effort.' In fact, you couldn't even be bothered to leave the movie when the turn started."

"It all happened so fast . . ."

"I have no further questions for you, young man, but one of these days you may wish to ask them of yourself. They won't be easy to answer, I can assure you."

This was the wrap-up. Harry knew for certain he would be handed over for court-martial. If he had hoped Cutter might exert some pressure on the court members, it was clear by now that the Admiral had either been unsuccessful or chosen not to exert that pressure. The statements made ran full against him. There could be no mistaking the attitude of the court members.

Diane studied Harry during that final session. That morning the Admiral had flown up from Washington and told her the case was closed. There would be no reprieve for Harry. If Harry chose to reveal the other aspect of his assignment to the destroyer, he would be silenced. If he persisted, he would be imprisoned and tried again, this time under the National Security Act. As far as any theories of Slattery's possible misdemeanors were concerned, the Pentagon dismissed them out of hand. If Slattery was guilty, he was now dead. Slattery's case was closed. The Truxton Cipher folder was closed. Cutter was to tell all that to Harry after this session.

Hawk was thoroughly enjoying himself. Pointedly he directed a new line of questioning at *Argonne*'s handsome Commanding Officer. For just as Hawk now lusted after Harry's scalp, he also wanted his brother captain to go scot-free. There was only one party in the room responsible for the collision. Justice would be served with Harry's court-martial; there was no need to embarrass further the honorable officer now before him. Because of the enormous loss of life, Hawk knew that the only grounds for criticism of *Argonne* lay in the manner in which the rescue operation had been carried out. Therefore, he directed his final questioning into that area.

"In your own words, Captain, would you please tell us the measures you took to rescue the crew of *Somerset*?"

A shaft of yellow sunlight struck *Argonne*'s Commanding Officer as he faced the court. He sat erect in his chair, dressed in extravagant, newly pressed whipcords, his braid and gold buttons flashing in the light, his campaign ribbons a silent testimony to the experience behind his careful, precise replies. His eyes flashed alertly. His manner spoke well of him. Here was a man who had earned the right to command a massive vessel, to lead a crew that numbered in the thousands. His composure was in marked contrast to the demeanor of the young Lieutenant Commander who slumped beside him.

"I am sure, sir, that you are aware of the measures spelled out in Naval Regulations to mitigate loss of life in the event of collision at sea. I was, of course, on the bridge at the moment of collision. As already noted, my vessel was backing down under full emergency power. I called away the rescue party immediately following the collision and ordered my crew to stand to quarters. I caused my vessel to be lighted. I informed the rest of the formation that I was maneuvering independently to effect rescue and I requested other ships in the area to stand clear. As I recall, there was some small confusion at the time because one of the destroyer's crewmen, the Chief here before you, was seen dangling from the starboard gallery of my ship. I ordered my First Lieutenant to carry out Nielson's rescue. Then I placed four boats in the water, two on each side, a hospital corpsman in each boat, and I ordered the boats to carry out expanding-square searches in the area of the collision." He glanced apologetically at Harry. "I'm afraid that there wasn't a great number of survivors. When the four boats returned . . ."

"Five, wasn't it?" Harry interjected the question without warning.

Argonne's Commanding Officer looked to Hawk for guidance. Hawk's reply was testy. "*I'm* asking the questions, young man."

"Yes, sir, but *Somerset*'s whaleboat *was* in the water."

"Mr. St. John, if you interrupt again, I'll have you removed from this room." Hawk's manner gave every indication that he meant what he said. "Disregard the question, Captain. Please continue."

Pozo King stared helplessly at the three court members. "I'm sorry, Captain Hawk, but it's already in the record."

"Well, then, strike it out."

"I can't, sir. Every question and every response must be entered in the transcript."

Exasperated, Hawk waved a delicate hand in the air. "Oh, very well, then. Captain, please answer the question."

"I recovered four boats and that was all. You are mistaken, Commander. *Somerset*'s boat went down with the ship."

"Are you absolutely certain of that, Captain?" Harry asked the question with an air of suppressed excitement.

"Of course I'm certain. Four boats went out and four came back—all from my command."

"You had no missing boat crews?"

"Definitely not. Look here, if you are suggesting that *Somerset*'s boat was in the water and we missed it, then I am afraid you are wrong, Commander. We stayed in the area until first light, and I personally supervised the final radar sweeps before ordering the course for home. There was nothing afloat out there." He added an afterthought: "Would that there had been."

"Hear, hear," mumbled Lord.

"I think this has gone far enough." Hawk consulted his watch. "Also, I think we have just about concluded this preliminary hearing. I am satisfied that we have made a complete and detailed exploration of the events leading up to this unfortunate incident. I would like to conclude this preliminary hearing today. Gentlemen, unless there are any further questions . . ."

MacDonald hoisted aloft the stem of his pipe. "Yes, I have one last question."

Hawk shrugged his shoulders. "Very well, sir."

MacDonald fixed Harry with a cold, unwavering stare. The man's bluff integrity cut through to the soul with the intensity of a laser beam. Harry knew that MacDonald's vote would be decided by his answer to this last question.

"Commander St. John, I want you to tell me if *you*

still think you did all within your power to avert the collision that cost the lives of most of your shipmates. Just look me in the eye and answer Yes or No."

Harry took a deep breath and glanced around the small room. All eyes were fixed upon him. He turned back to MacDonald, his answer firm and clear.

"Sir, under the protection afforded me by the Fifth Amendment to the Constitution, I respectfully decline to answer that question on the ground that my answer might incriminate me."

Harry watched distaste form over the old seaman's features. His words quite loud in the shocked stillness, MacDonald replied, "I misjudged you, lad. May God have mercy upon you."

Sixteen

Like surf battering the shore, repeated peals from the telephone broke upon Harry's sleep. His fist groped for the receiver. The glowing hands of the bedside clock stood close to five in the afternoon. Cradling the telephone against his ear, he croaked a sleepy hello.

"Sorry if I woke you, Commander." The words seemed to come all in a rush. "Name's Henry Hunter—from J.A.G. I wonder if I could see you for a moment."

"Yeah, sure," he replied, not sure at all. "Come on up." The line went dead, and he was left staring sleepily at the black receiver. He shook his head, hung up, and lurched into the bathroom. A splash of cold water in the face helped. He tucked in his shirt and padded to the door just as his visitor knocked once, quite softly, on the thin plywood partition.

Lieutenant Hunter was short and stocky, a regular Mister Five-by-Five. He took off his cap and allowed a lock of brown hair to fall onto his forehead.

"Did Commander King tell you I was coming?"

"No."

Lieutenant Hunter smiled easily. "Oh, then I'm doubly sorry." Social deception—not sorry at all, Harry thought. "May I have ten minutes?"

"Sure. Come on in. Bourbon or Scotch?"

"Neither, thanks. I understand you are supposed to meet Admiral Cutter in a few minutes, so I'll make my business short."

"How do you know I'm supposed to meet Admiral Cutter?"

"He told me. In fact, he helped assign me to your case. Commander King was supposed to have told you."

"Assigned you? As what?"

"Defense counsel."

"Oh, I see. You mean, because of this afternoon?"

Hunter sighed. "Look, Commander, if you are still offering, maybe I will have an inch of Scotch. Perhaps you had better have some too."

Harry lit a cigarette and quickly mixed two drinks. "All right, shoot. Give it to me straight."

"J.A.G. assigned me to your case last week. I've read the entire proceedings to date. It's interesting reading."

"Thanks."

"You haven't a chance."

"That opinion and fifteen cents will get you a cup of coffee. Where do you fit in?"

"At the end of the beginning. Look, the way things stand, you are a cinch to draw a general court-martial. King has already drawn up the specifications, in fact."

"I know. I saw them. So?"

"So J.A.G. wants you to have legal counsel *now*. You drop that Fifth Amendment silliness. During the court-martial—which will be fast—we stress your lack of recent sea experience. We stick to the illness angle. Anyone can make a mistake—it certainly wasn't intentional. Also, we come down hard on your extra efforts to improve the ship. You are still on the hook, but only half on. I'll try and make a deal with the court—maybe as light as a stiff reprimand, at worst a little time in a naval prison." Hunter correctly read the expression on Harry's face. "Look," he added, "the Navy wants this thing over with. It's damned hard on morale."

"And the Navy image?"

"Damned hard on that too, I can assure you."

"Earlier you said that Admiral Cutter helped assign you to my case. Why Cutter? He's not in J.A.G."

Hunter's eyes regarded him coolly over the rim of his liquor glass. "He's taken a special interest in this case." Harry noted that Hunter sat very straight in his chair. Despite his bulky size, his movements were precise, almost dainty.

"*Why* has he taken a special interest in my case?"

"I don't know. I've heard rumors that O.N.I. is mixed up in this. If so, I don't want to know anything about it. I won't take the case otherwise. I think I can get you off with a minimum of fuss on a straight plea of guilty. I think you would be wise to take that route." He tossed off the contents of his glass and stood up. "Think it over. I'll be in the B.O.Q. for another few days—just next door, in fact. I'll look in later tonight."

When the door had closed, Harry made straight for the telephone. The Defense Department Locator was still open in Washington, and he didn't have long to wait before a bored operator came on the line to help him.

"You don't even have the middle initial," she complained. "It's a common name. I have seven Lieutenant Henry Hunters listed."

"This one would be stationed in Washington."

"Well, I have two. One stationed in the Defense Supply Agency, and one in the office of the Chief of Naval Operations." She giggled. "We're not supposed to say exactly where in his case."

"None in J.A.G.?"

"None listed. You want me to ring one of the two?"

"I guess not, Operator. I made a mistake. Thanks."

He hung up thoughtfully. Half an hour later he made one other phone call—this one to Lieutenant Jacoby at the Newport Base Hospital. But Jacoby couldn't answer his question without first checking the hospital records. He flicked up the intercom button that connected him to the floor nurse.

"Miss Longford, look up the frequency and dosages of Tuinal issued to a Lieutenant Halliday over the past few months. And hurry, please; I've someone waiting on the phone."

"Yes, Doctor. However, would you first authorize an out-of-town visitor to see the multiple-fracture case in two-oh-six? It's . . . ah . . . past regular visiting hours."

"That's Perrelli, isn't it? Sure . . . He's okay . . . he's being sent, cast and all, to the reassignment pool tomorrow. Now hurry and dig out that Halliday record."

Miss Longford turned to the bulky man hovering at her desk and handed him an admittance slip. "Go ahead, Mr. Hunter. If anyone challenges you, show them that card."

However, as he would have suspected, no one challenged Henry Hunter. The rest of the staff was far too busy practicing the medical profession to even notice him. Hunter found Perrelli's room at the end of the long corridor. The radarman was flat on his back, hard at work blowing smoke rings toward the ceiling.

"Perrelli? The name's Hunter." He extracted his wallet and flipped it open to his I.D. "I'm with O.N.I., and I'd like to ask you a few questions."

Perrelli's eyes widened. He pushed himself upright and dropped the cigarette into a half-empty coffee cup.

"You come here to draw up charges against that creep Dieter?"

"Not really. Mostly I wanted to ask you about the collision."

Perrelli scratched his crotch and regarded Hunter warily. "You are talking to the wrong guy. I wasn't even there."

"That's what I wanted to talk to you about. I was told that in your job in the Combat Information Center you used to pretty well run the ship—tell the bridge what course to steer, speed to use, that sort of thing. That correct?"

"Yeah, I guess so."

"And you were so good at it that you were virtually irreplaceable?"

"Best in the Fleet," responded Perrelli modestly.

"No, I mean that if you weren't on the radar that night there really wasn't anyone who could take your place."

"So?"

"So I'm suggesting that had you been there, it's possible the accident wouldn't have occurred."

"One thing's for sure: that radar wouldn't have gone out."

"Did you ever before have trouble with the radar?"

"In a rough sea the antennae would salt up sometimes."

"But it was calm that night, wasn't it?"

"Yeah—that's what I never understood."

"And Dieter: did you ever fight with him before?"

"No, I hardly knew him."

"I understand that you fought with him over a Miss Gloria Faboola. Is that correct?"

"Yeah. She pronounces it *Fab*ula." He accented the first syllable. "Dieter said he had a date with her."

"Miss Fabula told me that she had never set eyes on him before that night. Can you explain that?"

"You mean he picked a fight with me for no reason at all?"

"Looks that way. Unless you can think of a reason why."

"The only thing I can think is what a lucky bum he is."

"Lucky? But he was killed on the ship."

Spider Perrelli regarded his visitor coolly. "That's why I think he's lucky," he replied.

Rain clotted with sleet spattered the windshield as Harry eased the Ford into the almost-deserted parking lot behind the King's Inn. He sprinted through the slush that had already accumulated on the parking apron that led to the small taproom at street level. The elegant hostelry, a century-old monstrosity of Victorian gingerbread, had several dining and drinking areas, but only the small off-street bar and main dining room were kept open at this time of year.

It was very much like Cutter to stay at the King's Inn. A man of Cutter's generation would find charm in the soaring archways, the sweeping verandas, the ancient staff, almost as run-down as the Inn itself. Harry, on the other hand, found the place majestically pretentious and enormously dull. However, for a meeting place it would at least have the virtue of solitude. No one in his right mind would come to the King's Inn on a night like this.

Cutter, dressed in civilian tweeds, sat at the far end of the taproom, studying the outside world through the leaded glass panes that fronted on Prince Street. Behind him, a roaring wood fire lit the scrubbed oak floor, the polished black mahogany of the elegant bar, and the half dozen prints of clashing frigates that battled it out across the walls of the taproom. Cutter sipped Dry Sack and absently nibbled on London biscuit. When he spied Harry, he signaled quickly to the waiter.

"Old Fashioned do it, St. John?"

"Yes, sir. I think I earned a drink tonight just getting here."

The Admiral placed the order and observed, "You look fit, St. John."

"Don't let appearances fool you. I'm done in. I had a spare uniform in the car. Everything else I own went down with the ship."

"I understand things have gone rather poorly for you."

"Couldn't be worse. Who told you? Hunter?"

If Cutter was surprised at Harry's mention of the Lieutenant, he didn't show it.

"No. I talked to King for a few minutes. He met me at the plane and brought me up to date. Who is Chief Nielson, and what does he have against you?"

"Nielson made a mistake, that's all. I'm glad that you at least weren't taken in." Harry explained briefly what had happened on *Somerset*'s bridge just before the collision. "Slattery had a purpose in mind behind all of his actions that night. I can understand why Nielson might have been confused."

"I see," the Admiral replied in a manner that suggested that he didn't "see" at all. "Harry, I wanted to talk to you . . ." The waiter arrived with St. John's Old Fashioned, and Cutter allowed the sentence to dangle. Harry sensed that whatever the Admiral had on his mind, it wasn't going to be easy to say. A hint of careful planning lay behind this too-casual beginning. Harry decided to take the initiative.

"Have you seen the evening papers, Admiral?" Harry held up a copy of the late-evening edition of the *Providence Courier*. DESTROYER DISASTER OFFICER TAKES FIFTH screamed a bold headline on the front page. "They really gave me a great roasting," Harry laughed. "The account sent over the wire services is almost as gory."

"I see no cause for amusement, Commander. Your little theatrics this afternoon did you no credit."

"Ah, but that's because there's so much you don't know."

"*I* don't know?" Cutter's tone was sarcastic. He turned up both palms expectantly.

Harry tossed off half of his drink, grateful for the burning sensation that cut across the chill in his body.

"I think I know what you came up here to tell me,"

he replied. "You were going to say, 'Sorry about the fix you're in, but the case is now closed.' Since Slattery and the ship are gone, you can cross off the possibility of *Somerset* as the source of the Truxton Cipher compromise. In effect, you were going to tell me not to count on you to pull my chestnuts out of the fire. Am I right?"

The Admiral smiled bleakly. "I wouldn't have used exactly that language."

"No. I'm sure you would have been much more graceful. But please remember, I lost a ship once before. There's nothing like a little court of inquiry to make a man feel all alone in the world. However, this time I don't intend going down."

Cutter studied Harry's face carefully. "Go ahead. What do you plan to do?"

Harry drained his drink and signaled the barman for a refill.

"I'm afraid I'm tired of fighting everyone's battles and winding up the only loser. I know for a fact that Slattery was up to his neck in espionage. I don't know all of his accomplices yet, but *I think I know how he carried it off.*"

The Admiral was now quite suddenly a different person. The familiar, cozy manner disappeared, replaced by a hard calculating shrewdness.

"So you see, we aren't yet quite ready to tie a nice little ribbon around the package," said Harry. "James lost, Slattery killed, St. John just an innocent bystander who finds himself up before a court of inquiry. Well, it won't wash. Now I need your help, and I'm going to get it. I want to be exonerated by that court that finished its inquiry today. That's my price, and you'll have to pay it if you expect my cooperation."

"But what can I do, Commander? Slattery's dead. The ship's gone. There's no remaining evidence. You are one of the few left alive. I'd thank my lucky stars for that."

Harry knew that the Admiral was much more worried

than he chose to let on. Nervously he tugged at his golden Annapolis ring and purred, "You had better just tell us all you know, Commander."

"Not without something from you first. I want you to go back to the Chief and tell him I need help. Once I have his promise to use influence on the court, I'll tell you *everything* I know."

"But the ship's lost. Slattery's dead. It's all over. Why should he help you?"

Harry spaced out his next words carefully. "Because, Admiral, it's not, as you say, *all* over. If I don't get a promise of help, I'm going to blow off the lid. The news media have been chasing me all over Newport. I might let them catch me. If I do, I could tell them the whole story of my assignment to *Somerset* as a decoy for a counter-intelligence operation that was ill conceived and clumsily mounted." He watched Cutter, unsure of the man.

"That aspect has no bearing on the loss of the ship. Besides, you really know nothing about it. You could only do great harm to the service." The Admiral's manner was contemptuous. He eyed Harry coldly.

"Admiral, I find I may be going to prison. I'm fighting for my life."

"If you go to prison for incompetence resulting in the loss of a fine ship and almost two hundred men, then it will be a fate which you richly deserve."

"The Guard dies, but never surrenders," Harry quoted; "the polite version of General Cambronne's remark at the Battle of Waterloo. What he actually said was *Merde!* And so do I."

"You do, do you?" said the Admiral coldly. And then in a coaxing tone he prompted, "You said you thought you knew something."

Harry withdrew the manila envelope from his pocket, extracted Slattery's Night Order Book, and handed it to Cutter. "This is just for openers, Admiral. It contains the only record of Slattery's espionage activities that I am aware of. It is, of course, written in Slattery's own hand."

"I still don't see what this has to do with your own problem."

"The two are interwoven. Admiral, what I'm going to tell you may be hard to believe, but it's the only rational explanation for the scattered events that have taken place since I joined *Somerset*."

"You sound a bit like a man grasping at straws, Commander."

Harry ignored the sarcasm. "First," he continued, "I believe that Slattery *was* the source of your security leak. I think that one way or another, Slattery regularly stole from Abel that coding equipment which *Somerset* carried in duplicate. I think he then put the equipment, a short-range beeper, and instructions for the next rendezvous into a plastic bag and had the package tossed over the side at the proper time. A small submarine, perhaps operating from one of the electronic snoopers off our coast, could then home in on the beeper and retrieve the package. That submarine was following us the morning we lost James. I saw its plot myself. I thought it was *Spikefish*. The plastic bag was probably coated with some sort of fluorescent material for night retrieval, and it most likely had a water-soluble plug. If not taken from the water within, say, two hours, the whole package would sink to the bottom. Probably there were standard rendezvous arrangements in the event the bag was not picked up. I think this book provided instructions to an accomplice aboard *Somerset* on just when to place the bags in the water."

Cutter stared at Harry, disbelief etched into his expression. "Show me the instructions."

"Look here." Harry flipped open the water-swollen pages. "The time we can expect to vary, but most likely to be after nightfall. It would then be a simple matter for a man to drop such a package from the ship. Because *Somer-*

set could be expected to be in various formations and with various combinations of boilers and engines operating to give various speeds, I ruled out those possibilities. Also, the weather is variable and could not be depended upon for conveying a simple instruction. No, the only way in which Slattery could get his message across would be either in the way he signed his name, or in variations to the standard instructions he gave each night to the Officer of the Deck. And remember that this is a book that sits open on the chart table twenty-four hours a day for all the crew to see. Anyone could stroll up and read the book without arousing curiosity. In fact, he'd only be doing what he was supposed to be doing—familiarizing himself with the instructions of his Commanding Officer."

"You forgot one thing, Commander," Cutter interrupted. "He could never take the chance such a package would be sucked back toward the screws and seen by the fantail watch."

"I didn't forget that, Admiral. The platform from which the package was deposited in the water was *outboard* of the ship. Read the instructions for the dates on which Abel and James were lost."

He handed the book to Cutter. The Admiral adjusted his spectacles and began to read aloud the portions of the book that Harry had underlined.

"Night of January thirteenth . . . Torpedo Exercise Zulu Fifteen scheduled to be carried out during the eight-to-twelve watch. . . . Ship's coxswain has permission to swing out and repair the whaleboat, all work to be completed by oh-one-hundred-fifteen. . . . Night of February twenty-fifth . . . Steaming independently with no exercises planned . . . Ship's coxswain has permission to swing out and work on the whaleboat, all work to be completed by oh-six hundred . . ." The Admiral looked up. "I can't believe it. This is just coincidence. How about the night of collision? There could be no such package in water about to be searched carefully for survivors. These instructions also call for swinging out the boat." Cutter tapped the book.

"That's right, Admiral. But there was another use for the boat on that night. You'll notice that there is no time shown. That's because there was no transfer scheduled that night. Instead, the boat was to be cut free just before the collision. *Somerset* didn't wind up under *Argonne*'s bows because of blunders on anyone's part. The entire 'accident' was planned by a man who knew it was going to happen and therefore had an excellent chance of escaping. All he had to do, in fact, was have the whaleboat cut free and dive after it just before the collision. The whole thing was planned in detail right down to the theft of the ship's cash. Admiral, you pressed him too hard. Slattery was desperate. He could see what was coming. Admiral, I'm telling you that Duke Slattery deliberately ran *Somerset* under the carrier's bows!"

The Admiral shook his head. "I can't believe it," he said.

"You can believe it. Slattery's alive, and so is his accomplice. Furthermore, I think I know where they are!"

Seventeen

"You look like the central character in a Shakespearean tragedy."

Harry smiled and tossed off the contents of his balloon glass of cognac. Above the Happy Hour chatter in the officers'-club bar, a tape of the Tijuana Brass told the story of the Spanish flea.

"Diane, he said he'd pass along what I told him tonight."

She covered his hand with her own. Hating herself, she said, "Harry, you can't believe that story."

"I don't know what I believe. The news media are screaming for my head; I'm starting to get hate mail; and I've become the *cause célèbre* for the lunatic fringe. You're the only good thing that has happened to me in the past few months."

"But Cutter's with you too!"

"I shook him up. I know that. He doesn't know what to think now. The man's worried. He'll have to help me."

"Worried men are dangerous men."

"That cuts both ways. I'm worried too."

She sighed. "You persist in thinking you can take on the

entire naval establishment." She glanced at her watch. "Look, I've simply got to get back. Will you call for me after my watch is over?"

"Of course. I'll take you back now."

Outside, it was sharply cold and brilliantly clear. An Arctic north wind, sweeping flocks of Canadian geese before it, shattered any illusion of an early spring and confirmed the forecast of an imminent snow. He couldn't have ordered a better night for his purpose. They said goodbye at the Operations Center, and he walked quickly down the hill to the B.O.Q. A Marine sergeant waited for him in the lobby.

"Mr. St. John?" The Marine looked embarrassed.

"Yes, Sergeant?"

"I was ordered to deliver this to you personally, sir. I'll need your signature on the copy."

He handed Harry a typewritten order signed by the Base Executive Officer. Effective on receipt, the order restricted Harry to the B.O.Q., the officers' club for meals, and the Naval War College. He was forbidden to enter other areas of the base, visit units of the fleet, or leave the base. He wasn't arrested yet, but this was almost the same. Granted that he was only restricted, but considering his present circumstances, it was an order to be complied with. The Vice Admiral had picked up his gauntlet sooner than Harry had anticipated. He initialed the paper and returned it to the Marine.

"Okay, Sergeant; what's next?"

"A steward has been assigned to accompany you whenever you leave the B.O.Q. You're not to leave without him. Sorry about this, sir."

"Not your fault, Sergeant. You didn't write the order."

But that settled it. He'd have to act fast now. There was no one he could trust. In his room, he quickly changed clothes and gathered together the equipment he would need. He debated calling Diane, but decided against it. No one must know. He dashed off a short note to her and gave it to Amos to deliver. Lieutenant Henry Hunter was his problem now, and Harry didn't have much time. He grabbed up pillows, towels, and blankets and stuffed them into the bathrobe issued to him at the hospital. The result was just satisfactory: a crude dummy, which he placed in a chair in the darkest corner of the room. The stuffed bathrobe would do little more than suggest a lounging St. John, but that would be enough. He pulled up a chair and waited.

Hunter walked with the short, mincing steps some heavy people adopt. He was almost upon the door before Harry heard him. The Lieutenant stopped and waited for what seemed an eternity. Finally he rapped once, lightly.

"St. John . . . you up? Hunter here."

"Come on in. It's unlocked."

The door swung open. Harry waited until the Lieutenant was well inside, leaning forward to make out the figure in the corner, before he said softly, "Hank?"

Startled, Hunter pirouetted around off balance. Harry put all of his strength behind a fist which caught his visitor full on the chin. With one faint *clop,* Hunter went over backward, half onto the bed. Softly, Harry closed the door behind him. He stretched the Lieutenant full out on the bed and rolled him over. From a holster worn at the small of his back, Harry removed and pocketed Hunter's snub-nosed .38-caliber revolver. He fished out the man's wallet and flipped it open. Hunter's identification card was unlike the regular officer's I.D. It identified Henry Hunter as an intelligence officer. "J.A.G., huh!" said Harry. The Lieutenant's pulse and respiration were slow but steady. A small trickle of blood coursed from a corner of his mouth. Harry turned out the light, softly raised the window, and climbed out on the fire escape.

Frozen snow came away under his boots in small crusts that fell softly to the ground below. There was ice on the teetering steel frame. Halfway down, he slipped and came close to falling. The rusted metal rattled alarmingly. Finally he reached the ground and, keeping to the shadows, moved quietly in the direction of his car. A blast of cold air rattled the building and sent small shards of dry snow flying through the air. Somewhere in the distance a car's engine started. A door slammed inside the building, and he heard the sound of noisy laughter. At last he reached the car and started up the engine. He drove quickly but carefully over the slippery roads to the main fleet landing. It took twenty minutes, and he was almost too late.

While Harry had been waiting for Hunter to knock on his door, Admiral Cutter was ordering Diane to pull the small Fiat off the road just before they reached the main gate of the naval station.

"What is it? I thought I was to take you to the airport."

"I've changed my mind."

"I haven't much time," the girl snapped. "I'm supposed to be on duty."

"You'll be all right. Your friend Harry knows just a little too much. He was overeager to get me out of the way tonight. Even if I caught that plane to Washington, he must know that I wouldn't have time to stop the court from announcing its findings tomorrow morning. I don't think our seafaring friend intends showing up for that session tomorrow. I think he's going to look for Slattery tonight. I told you O.N.I. put a man in the room next door to him without even consulting me. I think I'll check to see that St. John's tucked in for the night."

A flashlight illuminated the interior of the car. "You know you can't stop here, Miss; you're blocking the entrance," complained the Marine who guarded the gateway. Then he caught sight of the Admiral's identification card. With a thundering crash of shoe leather, the Marine snapped to attention and saluted.

"That's all right, son. We'll only be here a moment. Do you have a telephone in there?"

"Yes, sir."

"Diane, pull in behind the guard shack and wait for me." His mind made up, the Admiral followed the Marine into the small building that controlled access to the naval base.

A half hour later, the phone rang urgently in Shore Patrol headquarters at the fleet landing, just as Harry strolled casually past it. Someone up at Base Operations had thought fast. Harry hadn't counted on that. Aquidneck Island was just that: an island. If you wanted to catch someone, the first step would be to watch the obvious exits: the two bridges and of course the fleet landing. It was Harry's luck that the Duty Officer's first call was to the exact spot that Harry had chosen. A moment after he stepped out on the dock apron, Shore Patrol pounded out of the small waiting room behind him. Quickly they sealed off the dock area, pushing together the sailors from the *Argonne* who were returning from shore leave. Then one of the patrol spotted the Ford in the almost-empty parking lot. A great shout went up. Desperately, Harry pressed forward.

"*Argonne, Argonne* . . . departing!" the loud-hailer blared as the boat dispatcher, unaware of what was taking place, kept to his normal schedule. Despite orders from the Shore Patrol, several dozen drunken sailors pressed forward to a large motor launch. The loud-hailer blared again —this time an officious command to, "Belay that last announcement . . . All hands, *stand fast!*" One petty officer close to Harry muttered, "Goddammit, why don't they make up their minds?" The sailors roared their annoyance and continued to press forward to the pier. Harry let himself be carried along through the last chain-link fence. Confused, the sailors now spilled from the pier into the waiting motor launch, despite the half dozen angry patrolmen who tried to stop them. Harry stepped from the circle of light that framed this momentary confusion at the launch and sprinted desperately up the pier. He was trapped now unless there was another way off the pier.

Luck was with him. The Captain's gig from *Argonne* rocked gently against the rotting timbers, unattended while its crew went in search of hot coffee. Frantically, Harry cast off bow and stern lines. He leaped aboard. The boat was not as familiar to him as less lordly small craft, but the key was in the starter alongside the wheel, and the rest was obvious. He thumbed over the key, and the starter ground. An instant later, a pair of magnificent three-hundred-horsepower diesels roared into life. A yell of outrage from down the pier ended in an orange burst and the flat *wham* of a .45. The woodwork above him erupted in a shower of splinters. In one smooth motion he ducked, slammed home the gearshift, opened up the throttle, and twisted the wheel.

It was a magnificent little boat. Almost instantly the craft rose up on its keel and he was heading at full gallop for Goat Island. Another shot rang out. Harry came left at full speed into the midst of three yachts moored just off the lush elegance that is the Newport Yacht Club. Behind him he heard another boat engine start up. There were no more shots.

He eased back on the throttle. The boat was slamming through the small harbor waves, throwing great gouts of water to either side, and would make better speed with a lower throttle setting. He had been fantastically fortunate. The boat had more than enough power to outrace anything in the Navy's fleet of small patrol craft. Further, now they would *have* to come and get him. If for nothing else, *Argonne*'s Commanding Officer would have planes aloft at first light seeking his pride and joy.

He took Fort Adams close to port and hugged the southwestern end of Aquidneck Island. He found the control for the instrument lights and switched them on, but did not touch the running lights. A small electric heater came on automatically and soon began to warm the cabin. Gratefully, Harry shed his bulky overcoat. He lit a cigarette and forced himself to relax.

Above him, the stars flashed cold brilliance upon a choppy sea. To his left, the great brooding mansions along Ocean Point Road stared seaward with bluff, weathered faces. Ahead the way was clear, the sea-lanes deserted except for the distant red wink of the truck lights from some luckless destroyer on night operations. Soon he heard the soft, irregular clamor of the bell buoy marking the entrance to Narragansett Bay. He took departure on the buoy, coming right to south-southwest, the course to Block Island.

Slowly the boat's motion changed as he left behind the confused chop of the channel and entered the long reach of the ocean. The sleek craft began to pound the seaward side of the long crests, and a chilling spray splashed the cockpit. Again he slowed the diesels until the boat's motion told him that it rode easier over the long swells. He checked the fuel tanks and found them almost full—more than enough reserve for what he had in mind. Then he turned to his own final preparations.

Steering with an elbow hooked through the wheel, he retrieved the can of shoe polish from his coat. He had some difficulty rubbing on the coloring; the wax was cold and broke into thick, greasy chunks. But at last he was finished—all of his exposed skin now as dark as the night around him. He removed Hunter's revolver from his pocket.

The ugly weapon was in superb condition. The cylinder was full, and there was one oily round in the chamber. He would have preferred a heavier weapon, but the .38 would be just adequate given his advantage of surprise. Satisfied, he put on the gun's safety catch and returned the loaded revolver to his pocket. Now he had nothing to do but wait.

Thoughtfully, Diane read the brief note:

I think Slattery's alive. I'm going for him. I'll need help. Tell the Duty Officer he can find me on Block Island at a place called Dennison Point. All love—Harry

Around her the usually serene night watch had erupted into a frenzy of activity. Phones rang again as fast as they were put down. A strange officer with an angry discoloration on his jaw had appeared mysteriously to supervise the preparations for the search now about to start. The Officer of the Watch, an unhappy lieutenant, was pleased to divest himself of any further responsibility that night. He had enough trouble on his hands right now.

"But, sir, I simply don't know how he managed to steal the boat." On the other end of the telephone line, the Base Executive Officer said something rude.

"Christ, sir, *I* don't run that fleet landing. Tell him we're doing our best to find his boat. . . . Uh, yes, sir . . . just a moment." He placed a sweating palm over the instrument and looked helplessly at the girl.

"Lieutenant, would you check the DesLant operating schedule? His Nibs wants to know if we have any vessels operating off the mouth of the Bay tonight."

Diane hurried to a large plastic display hung at the far end of the room on which was kept the up-to-the-minute status of the hundred or so vessels assigned to the Newport area. Quickly she read through the list of grease-pencil inscriptions.

"The *T.R. Allen* is scheduled for night operations with a submarine from New London," she announced.

"Oh, God, no," groaned the Duty Officer. "The *Allen* will be way out in the submarine operating areas. Anything else?"

"Well, yes . . . *Pickering* is scheduled for a full-power trial tonight."

The Duty Officer fairly danced with ecstasy. He picked up the phone.

"We *are* in luck, sir. *Pickering* is making a full-power run. She probably would have started around ten tonight. My guess is she's building up and more than likely heading for sea room. Want me to divert her? . . . *Yes,* sir." Pleased with himself, he hung up the phone.

"Lieutenant, can we raise *Pickering* on voice radio?"

"Yes, sir. Right there in the Communications Center." She indicated the room adjoining them.

A few minutes later, the Duty Officer returned wearing a self-satisfied expression. "That fellow certainly kicked up a storm tonight," he observed. "But all's well now. *Pickering* will pick him up in two hours if he heads out to sea. If he tries to get ashore, the police are watching the coast. My God, I hope those damned reporters don't tumble to this before he's caught. Proper lot of fools we'd look like. He must have been loony to pull a stunt like this. Well, nothing to do now but wait it out." He flopped back on a battered leather sofa and closed his eyes wearily.

Diane looked once more at the message in her hand. The Admiral had told her they were probably off the island by now. But she couldn't chance it. It was either the Admiral or Harry. She had protected Cutter thus far; she would have to do so one more time. Quite deliberately, she tore the note in half, letting the pieces flutter into the paper sack of waste code strips that were collected and burned every hour.

Eighteen

The first snow flurries struck as Harry rounded Sandy Point. He throttled back so that the noisy spatter of the diesels would be less likely to announce his presence. The advancing snow front had warmed the air, but at the cost of visibility. By the time he was abreast of Great Salt Pond, the full force of the snow squall struck. He was forced to estimate his position from Dicken's Point and steer by compass. He consulted his watch. Two miles to go at a speed of ten knots. The downwind run would take exactly twelve minutes. When he looked up, Dicken's Point was blotted from view by a white curtain. The faint cabin light illuminated great wet flakes of falling snow. He switched off the cabin light, quickly regretting the loss of the heater at his feet. He thawed out his last bar of chocolate and devoured it hungrily.

Slattery's cove, as best he could recall, was slightly north of Dicken's Point. However, he wanted to approach the cove from the south. From downwind was the way the hunter approached his quarry, and from the south was the way that Slattery had found the cove in the first place.

It was almost two in the morning when he finally throttled back, shifted into neutral, and came hard left on the wheel. Slowly the boat coasted closer to the island. Through the snow, he heard the gentle slap of waves breaking over the boulders strewn at the base of the cliff. He could see nothing ahead but a white curtain. Then, just as he thought the boat must ground, a grayness caught his eye.

Looming out of the storm, the great brooding bluffs of Denison Point swam eerily into view. He came left on the wheel. Once around and heading upwind, he shut down the engine and coasted slowly along the faint whiteness of the shore. He was now only ten yards off the base of the cliff, and barely moving. The snow deadened every sound. He might as well have been alone in the universe.

If Slattery was alive, then Harry would recover all of his lost chips in this one bold play. If Slattery was dead, then Harry was done for. The answer to his future lay just a few yards ahead through the swirling snow.

The boat coasted on silently, but now much more slowly. Then, with a soft scraping sound, it grounded. *Argonne*'s launch was firmly ashore, wedged between two smooth rocks just off the promontory circumscribing the southern boundary of the cove. Harry climbed out of the small cabin and walked through the snow on the foredeck. Silently he lowered himself over the side and into the water. Before the sea reached his waist, his feet were on the bottom. He waded ashore on numb feet and worked his way up through the sharp, barnacle-infested rocks until he reached the crest. Hugging the rocky surface, he raised his head over the seaweed-covered boulders.

There was no one there. Slattery's cove was deserted.

Harry rose to his feet, too stunned to swallow the bitter pill of this stinging defeat. He stumbled down to the sandy cove and searched it carefully with his flashlight. There was nothing there: no footprints to match his own, no mark where the gig might have been grounded—nothing. A few well-rusted beer cans from the previous summer and the charred remains of a small wood fire that had probably warmed the beer drinkers were the only signs that Slattery's cove had ever been visited by anyone before him.

But he couldn't have been wrong. He remembered the unusual number of equipment boxes that had been taken ashore the day the destroyer had stopped here, the track of the submarine that had followed them that day, and his fleeting glimpse of the gig on that terrible night. It had all added up in his own mind. He had been so certain. Now there was nothing left for him but the humiliating return to Newport.

Sick at heart, Harry kicked at the blackened faggots of the old campfire. A small scrap of paper, half burned, peeped from the edge of the ashes and charred wood. He picked it up and smoothed out the crumbling remains. It was part of a cash receipt—the sort of commercial nonsense one sacrifices gladly on a cool night. He started to throw it away, and then looked at it again. His heart began to pound. What a fool he had been. He had played right into their hands. The name of the payer was missing, but the receipt had been issued by the Foundation for the Advancement of International Non-Theatrical Events!

"For Christ'sakes, Captain, we just put that new firebrick in the boilers. You can't slow down now—the brick'll crack surer than hell! It's gonna take two hours to cool off that old plant." *Pickering*'s Chief Engineer, angry and flushed with the heat of his engine room, stood on the wildly swaying bridge in his shirt sleeves, the wind pulling at his hair. Behind him the destroyer's funnels streamed thick, oily black smoke, flecked with darting red sparks.

"I know. I know, Chief," soothed the Captain. "But orders are orders. We have to reschedule this run, I guess."

Pickering had been racing through the dark night at close to thirty-five knots when the mysterious order came, aborting the full-power trial. The old ship still throbbed wildly as her rebuilt engines drove them ahead at wide-open throttle. The Captain considered his engineer's complaint for a moment and then ducked into the pilothouse.

"How much right rudder you carrying to hold her one-eight-zero?"

"About two degrees, Captain," the helmsman responded.

"Very well. Put your rudder amidships and hold it there!"

"Rudder's amidships, Captain."

The Captain explained to his engineer: "Okay, no need now to slow for a turn. Without that two degrees she'll come left very slowly. I'll stop the swing when we're headed north. But I can give you no more than an hour. Start throttling down!"

"Well, I won't be responsible if anything happens to that firebrick," the engineer grumbled as he disappeared down the narrow ladder that led below to his glowing engine room. However, the Captain had more important worries.

"Passing one-five-five very slowly, sir," the Officer of the Deck said, anticipating the Captain's question.

"Very well. Steady zero-zero-zero when we come to it. What's it look like ahead?"

"I just checked the radar. There's a snow squall that starts at Block Island and goes inland. No shipping to speak of. But we'll have to slow down before we hit that snow."

The Captain sighed. "Tell *that* to the Chief Engineer. Any sign of the helicopter?"

"Not yet, sir. But he'd better get here before that snow, or his passenger's gonna have one hairy trip."

The passenger referred to, Henry Hunter, had no trouble spotting *Pickering* a few minutes later. The chopper had just burst out of the swirling squall when they saw the destroyer, two miles away and bearing down upon them at a fast clip.

"Gonna be a rough ride, Lieutenant," warned the pilot.

"That old scow's really tearing along. I got time for only one pass before the snow catches us."

Hunter grunted and fastened his harness. "Here's hoping there's a St. Bernard down there with a bottle of brandy. I'm gonna need it."

"You'll be all right. Just tell those swabs not to make the line fast once I drop you," the pilot cautioned. "Something about a sailor and a line—they can't just hold it; it's gotta be tied to something. I don't wanna follow them around all night on a thirty-foot leash."

With a swooping turn that crumpled Hunter into a corner of his seat, the pilot banked the helicopter over the small, dancing fantail of the destroyer and carefully adjusted his speed to match that of the ship. He edged slightly to port to avoid the heat streaming from her funnels. Then he grabbed the radio: "Hold it right there, *Pickering*." He pushed Hunter's shoulders. "Here come the goods!"

Hunter heard a cheerful "Goodbye!" and stepped out of the small hatch, to swing directly under the frigid wash of the chopper's blades. He felt himself slide frighteningly fast through the blackness until, with a sudden jerk, he dangled directly over the destroyer's stern, still towed below the chopper at close to forty miles an hour. He tried to stretch his legs down the tantalizingly small distance between his feet and the destroyer, but the fantail suddenly shot out from under him and he hung over the frothy wash of the ship. A muffled curse from the ship reached him a moment before a heaving line snaked over his shoulder. The throbbing fantail appeared to skew around under him again. With a sharp jolt, he found himself on all fours upon the cold, wet plating of *Pickering*. Quickly he unsnapped the harness before he was yo-yoed back aloft. The harness soared upward. He saw a hand wave at him from the open window of the chopper. Then the craft's exhaust flamed blue, and with a loud clatter the helicopter disappeared upward into the swirling snow. Someone helped him upright, and he found himself pushed along to the bridge. His teeth were chattering by the time *Pickering*'s Skipper met him with a steaming cup of coffee.

"Drink that, Lieutenant. Then maybe you'll be good enough to tell me what this is all about."

"C-can't t-tell you everything, sir." Shivering with cold, he dug under his windbreaker and fished out his wallet. He worked on the coffee while *Pickering*'s Skipper studied the plastic card under the chart-table light. Finally the Captain looked up and carefully compared Hunter's face with the I.D. photo. Except for a purple bruise on the Lieutenant's swollen jaw, the faces were the same.

"Okay, I'm satisfied. Now what's my ship got to do with O.N.I.?"

"We're looking for a man, Captain. He escaped from Newport tonight—never mind how, or why we want him. He's in a fast boat out here. We want to catch him. He's not to be hurt."

"You know where he is?"

Hunter stabbed a finger at the chart indicating Block Island and its surrounding waters. "That's where he was last headed. You can pick him up on radar, I suppose?"

"Hmmm . . . I don't think so. Look for yourself. Snow's left nothing but grass on the short scale."

It was true. For several miles radiating outward from the center of the scope, the return was blocked out by a green luminescence. The Captain snapped out an order, and *Pickering*'s twenty-four-inch searchlights suddenly probed the blackness ahead with great yellow fingers of light. "That'll be a help, but the snow's cut their usefulness too. Still, we can see a mile anyway." The Captain looked at Hunter curiously, but the expression on the Lieutenant's face discouraged further confidences. The Captain shrugged. "I'll zigzag, keeping between the Bay and the island. If he's out here, we'll know soon enough."

"I don't know about the lights. He'll see them."

"Mister, even for O.N.I. I don't run my ship through a snowstorm at full speed without lights. There's fishermen out here, you know." Contempt for the nonseagoing Navy edged into the Captain's tone. Hunter knew better than to argue.

They missed the boat on the run out to Block Island and then slowly retraced their course to Narragansett Bay. It was on the eastern leg of the final zigzag that they found him.

"Surface contact two-seven-zero," bawled the shivering port lookout. The bridge searchlight briefly illuminated *Argonne*'s launch as it plowed ahead through the heavy seas. As they watched, the small boat suddenly speeded up and turned for the mouth of the Bay.

"Damned fool's going to broach if he isn't careful," muttered the Captain.

"No, he won't. That man knows what he's doing."

"Want me to try a warning shot? That'll make him heave to."

"No. He wouldn't stop anyway. Pull up into the mouth of the Bay and we'll catch him as he comes in."

Pickering pulled ahead of the launch and a few minutes later slewed into position blocking the channel entrance to Newport. The dark bulk of Jamestown loomed to the west of them. The Captain studied the situation. "Mr. Hunter, we'll catch him if he comes this way. But if I were him, I'd just veer and take Jamestown to starboard in the west channel."

Hunter sighed. Their next move was obvious. "Not if you put your gig in the water and close off that entrance."

Pickering's Captain looked at him unpleasantly. "That would be just dandy, Lieutenant Hunter, but *Somerset* crushed our boat some weeks ago. *We don't have a gig!*"

As Hunter pounded the bridge coaming in frustration, Harry shot through the narrow gap and, still at full speed, steered the launch through the swirling snow into the west channel. They couldn't follow him there—the water was too shallow for *Pickering*. He eased off the throttle and worked the sleek boat north until the gray shadows of the Jamestown bridge appeared before him. Then he turned out of the channel and gently beached the boat. Within a few minutes snow had covered the launch until it was just another white lump on the landscape. Harry was safe from discovery until dawn. By then he could get a lift to Newport. There he knew what he must do.

"You're sure they'll catch him?"

Cutter put his hand on the girl's tense fist. "A matter of time, Diane. After all, where can he go? What can he say? The island's deserted." He glanced around the nearly empty officers' club. "Finish your nightcap, Diane, and I'll take you back." He wasn't that sure himself, though. He had risked being seen with the girl because he had to know everything that had happened that night in the Operations Center. Her report had been reassuring: everything still proceeding smoothly. Still, it was only prudent to guard against the unexpected.

"I wish this was over."

He studied her carefully. "I told you, he hasn't a chance. He knows nothing important—and more to the point, nothing that can be proved." Her concern worried him. "He's running for his life. Now he's discovered the island's deserted, he'll doubt his entire hypothesis."

"He may not."

"So? What if he doesn't? Where's the proof? He doesn't even know who's involved. Why, he even babbled out all he knows to me tonight—me, of all people!"

"It must have amused you." She said the words coldly.

"No, as a matter of fact, it didn't. He's a little too good, your dashing Fleet officer. But I'm a step ahead of him. Look here, do you think I *like* doing this?"

"I don't know. I just don't want him hurt. He's been hurt enough."

"Of course he won't be hurt. The game's over now. We've cooperated and that's the end of it. That was the bargain I made."

"I got you into this," she said miserably.

"Oh, Diane, we've been over that a thousand times. I was the one who made the first mistake."

But had it been his mistake? He had only followed the orders of his commodore. He paused, his mind leaping back once again to that moment in '42 when he had handed over the Truxton Cipher rotors to the Russians. Once back aboard his own ship, the Commodore hadn't lasted long enough to write that memorandum that would have absolved Cutter. And for the next six weeks Cutter had been radioless, his ship last reported as destroyed after having engaged the *Prinz Eugen*.

It had been the making of his career. In one of his fireside chats, Roosevelt had singled out the plucky destroyer that sacrificed itself to save the American convoy. How the Navy flacks had poured it on! Then, wonder of wonders, the old four-piper reappeared two months later, limping into Quincy with her one surviving officer so exhausted he had to be lashed to the binnacle.

What do you do? Stop the President as he's pinning the Navy Cross to your hospital sheets and say, "Oh, by the way, in order to warn that convoy I handed over our confidential code to the Russians eight weeks ago?" Do you ask the mayors of all the cities to rebag the confetti, roll up the ticker tape? Do you refuse to accept the Fast Carrier Task Force publicly given you by the President? If everyone assumes your message to the convoy was sent off *before* the radio room was shot out instead of *after,* why not let them?

Even then he could smell the change in the Washington climate regarding the Russians. Even if they believed the

Commodore had issued orders to hand over the code, he knew neither he nor the Commodore had had that authority. Why risk a cloud over the honors heaped upon him? Especially when he found out the rotors had been routinely rotated anyway and that set was now useless to the Soviet. But that was only his half of it.

They knew he would never cover for the Newport operation. Brutus was an honorable man. They waited till he was at sea before they approached the girl. They knew he hadn't reported the hand-over. The photographs, the devices themselves, the receipt he had foolishly countersigned were all they needed. Be exposed as a dupe of the Russians, or cooperate. A day was all Meek gave her. With the Admiral unreachable by phone, she was afraid to put anything into writing. In the end she had cooperated, and now he was forced to protect *her,* just as she had tried to protect *him*. But he would get them out of this yet.

"Don't worry, Diane. There's no evidence against us. Just give me a little more time."

"But the ship—all those men!"

"We can't bring them back to life now. Diane, it's *over*."

"And Slattery? What happens to him?"

"A hero—he'll be received as a hero!" That afternoon Dieter had casually referred to Slattery's destination as probably the Serbsky Institute of Forensic Psychiatry in Moscow, but he didn't tell her that. He knew about the Serbsky Institute. He would have to get Slattery out of there somehow.

"For his sake anyway, I'm glad."

"Will you trust your adopted *paterfamilias* for just another few days? By then this will all be over. You'll be out of it. Later we might even arrange St. John's release. Trust me!"

"I'm just tired. Of course I trust you."

He smiled at her then—an honorable man, gentle and kind, her adopted father. He couldn't tell her everything;

she would go to pieces. Because he sensed Hunter and O.N.I. were finally after him, he had to be doubly careful. St. John must be stopped at all costs. As a final precaution, he had loosed his one remaining accomplice to stop St. John if he succeeded in escaping the police and attempted to confront Meek. In that event, Cutter's orders were quite clear: kill St. John in any fashion, but kill him quickly and surely.

Nineteen

The ancient farm truck drew to a wheezing stop just beyond the bridge. The farmer leaned out and inspected Harry for a long moment before he was satisfied. "Hop in, fella. Going as far as town." The farmer had a red face, a long nose, and a Down East twang.

"That'll be just fine with me. Got caught in the snow last night. Had to run my boat ashore."

The farmer grunted in reply. As soon as Harry was settled beside him, the truck set off for Newport. They rattled along in silence until they had just entered town. Then, as if their conversation hadn't been spaced by twenty minutes of silence, the farmer said, "Some folk say Navy people make the worst sailors." He chuckled. "Knew you was Navy. Saw you beach the boat last night. Wouldn't pick up them hippie folks."

"Right here is fine. Thanks for the lift."

"No charge, young fella. Good day."

The coffee shop was steamy and empty of customers. Harry went right to the phone. After a short delay, he reached his party.

"Yeah, this is Perrelli." Over the phone the radarman's voice sounded somehow unfamiliar.

"Spider Perrelli? From *Somerset*?"

"That's right. Cosmo Perrelli in the flesh. Who's this?"

"Commander St. John."

"The hell it is!"

"It is. You can count on it. Perrelli, I need your help." The sharp crack of fast-breaking pool balls interrupted a long silence over the line. Apparently Perrelli had found life in the enlisted barracks not altogether unpleasant.

"Commander, you can drop dead for all I care. You read the papers this morning?"

"No."

"Well, you better. Man, you are on Page One. Half this town is looking for you. Did you really steal a launch?"

"Yes, I did. Now I need your help."

"Listen Commander, it's not like I got anything personal against you. Hell, I wasn't even on the ship that night. But you must be nuts. Every cop in town is out on the streets after you by now. I'm in enough trouble as it is."

"Perrelli, I didn't sink the ship."

"That isn't what the papers say."

"You'll have to take my word for it."

"Then what are you doing hiding out?" A note of crafty cunning crept into the radarman's voice. "Where are you, anyway?"

Harry realized that he wasn't getting anywhere with this approach. He tried a new tack. "How'd you like to settle your score with Dieter?"

"I'll flatten that crum. Hey, wait a minute. You telling me he's alive?"

"He's alive, all right," Harry replied grimly. "He had to get you out of the way. That's why he picked a fight with you."

"That bastard. I'll kill him."

"You can if you catch him. I know where he is."

Perrelli weakened. "You really steal that launch?"

"Can you get off base in the next few minutes?"

"Man, they don't even know I'm here. Best duty I ever had."

"Okay, Perrelli. Here's what I want you to do. . . ."

By the time the radarman rang off, two patrolmen had entered the coffee shop and were now, quite casually, looking over the patrons. Harry squeezed into a corner of the phone booth and continued talking into the dead line. With only the back of his head and the top of his sweater showing, he thought it unlikely they would take him for anything other than a fisherman from one of the trawlers at the nearby pier. But it was a long, tense moment before they left the shop. Everything hinged on the next hour. He couldn't afford to be caught; there was still no proof and too much to explain.

He paid for coffee and settled at an empty booth in which a morning newspaper had been abandoned. A large picture of Lieutenant Commander St. John, U.S.N., in dress uniform stared back at him from page one. The story made no mention of the note he had left Diane. That explained why he had been able to return to Newport that morning. The note had obviously never been delivered, and no one knew he was on Block Island. Except for the one dash through the swirling snow to escape *Pickering,* the seas had been deserted of the armada of pursuing small craft that he had expected. Clearly Base Operations did not yet know where he had gone, and that, unhappily, confirmed the logic of his new reasoning.

"I asked if you want cream. We don't usually serve coffee in the booths."

A waitress hovered over the table, pitcher in hand, scowl on face. She had a brassy, arrogant manner.

"I'm sorry. I didn't hear you. I don't want cream."

She continued to stare at him, glancing back and forth from his face to the newspaper spread out on the greasy table. Her hair was bleached a yellow, frizzled blond, but her eyes were bright with cunning. Embroidered on her spotted waitress uniform was a small *Amy* done in red thread.

"I said no, thanks."

"Sure, buddy, sure." She seemed anxious to prolong the conversation. The shop was now deserted except for the two of them. "We got fresh crullers and bismarcks in from Boston today. You look like you could use one. Warm you up, snow and all."

It was unhappily true that he was ravenous. It was also true that he was broke except for the small change that would finance this last transaction.

"No, thanks." He placed a dime and two nickels on the table. She shrugged and tossed a damp dish towel over her shoulder. She went back behind the counter and continued to study him closely. At last, her mind made up, she went to the telephone. He forced himself to finish the hot coffee, and only then did he gather up the newspaper and saunter out of the shop. By that time she was speaking rapidly on the phone.

Outside, there was bright sun overhead and wet slush underfoot. Once clear of the shop, he hurried away, stopping after a few blocks to stare into a store window as two policemen dashed by. He heard a siren in the distance, and ducking into a side street, he took a long, circuitous route away from the waterfront. A gust of cold air showered him with dry powdered snow. He shivered and walked faster, his breath coming in short, steaming bursts, his pores beginning to open. A few warmly clad pedestrians stared at him, but no one stopped him, and he was careful to stay in the middle of the crowds and away from the curbs.

He spotted the Volkswagen as he emerged from the crowded shopping plaza on Bellevue Avenue. Although he couldn't see the driver's face, something about the man's manner caught Harry's eye, the precise movements somehow vaguely familiar. He'd seen the man before, but without a good look at him now, he couldn't recall where or when they'd met. Harry heard the car's engine start as soon as he passed by. I'm jumpy, he thought—too nervous. No one on the street knew him, and of course if the V.W. driver had recognized him from the newspaper, he would simply have shouted for the police. Still, he was glad to see the little car waffle on past him through the slushy street as he waited for the WALK light at the next intersection. Except that the little car didn't go on. It stopped on the other side of the street along the route Harry was expected to take. The driver lit a cigarette and waited. The light changed, but Harry remained on the curb, undecided. He had a sixth sense of something not quite right.

"Come on . . . Come on! Holding us all up," a ruddy-faced man behind him complained. The snow had been plowed back against the curb, and only a small lane allowed pedestrians to cross to the next block. He couldn't stay there, and yet for some reason he didn't want to overtake the little Volkswagen. Finally he struck out at right angles to the street and headed for a small square across the way. He knew it was a mistake as soon as he reached the other side.

A Shore Patrol carryall was parked at one end of the square with its engine idling. Inside the cab, two bored petty officers methodically scanned the faces of passersby. Except for a small lane that led off at the opposite end, the park was for him a cul-de-sac. He walked rapidly down the diagonal, dodging children who had found a late-winter use for their sleds. The traffic light behind him changed. He heard the harsh toot of horns and from the corner of his eye saw the V.W. cut across traffic and start down the opposite side of the square. He could easily have turned back and retraced his steps, but when he glanced around, two patrolmen had turned onto the path and sauntered behind him. He hurried along, arriving at the corner just as the V.W. slowed down and stopped there, blocking his progress. The car window rolled down, and the man inside, without looking at him, hissed, "Quick, St. John, get in. The police are right behind you."

"Who are you?"

"Never mind that. Get in."

"No."

He heard the man sigh. The driver opened his door and got out. St. John finally recognized the dapper little man he had seen at Quonset Point. He was dressed just as tidily today, in a camel's-hair British walking coat with fur-lined lapels and a snappy chamois-skin cap that sported a large golden ornament with a thick brush. His shoes were patent leather and shone brightly in the wet snow.

"We met at the airport. Name's Ruben Silk. I offered you assistance then, and I'm offering it to you now."

"Why?"

"Listen, I don't have time to go into all the details. Those policemen will be here any minute."

He was nervous. His left eye kept twitching, and he kept his right hand in the pocket of his coat. He tried to smile, but it didn't quite come off.

"Why do you care if the police get here or not? I'm the one they're after."

"Listen, will you get in!"

"You seem awfully excited."

"Just do what I say."

"Perhaps the Foundation wouldn't want me to be picked up. Is that it? Are you with the Foundation?"

That registered. Despite Silk's attempt at self-control, one of his eyebrows rose at the mention of Meek's enterprise. Too late, he shrugged his shoulders in an unconvincing display of nonchalance, carefully estimating the remaining distance to the approaching police. Harry could now hear the crunch of the patrolmen's boots in the wet snow behind him. Silk turned as if to return to his place in the car.

"All right, you dumb shit. I told you I was a lawyer." Silk's right hand gently bulged the pocket of his expensive coat. "I was only trying to help."

Harry turned away quickly and made as if to get into the car with him. Before Silk moved to cover him, Harry drove his right fist full into the lawyer's stomach. With a sharp *phitt,* a small, blackened hole appeared in the center of the lawyer's pocket. Silk grunted quite loudly, then crumpled face down in the dirty snow. Footsteps pounded behind Harry.

"And what the hell's this?" boomed an Irish-inflected voice. Harry's arms were pinioned roughly behind him. "I saw you hit the poor lad."

Rubin Silk rose on one knee and retched in the snow. "Grab him first, officer," Harry warned. "You'll find a gun with a silencer in his right pocket. He just tried to shoot me."

The other patrolman, young and agile, yanked Silk's hand from his pocket. The gun fell out and landed in the snow with a soft squishy sound. The patrolman whistled softly. He studied Harry carefully for a moment and then lit up brightly. "Hey! Ain't you that Navy guy everybody's looking for?"

It was over at last. He was caught. He felt cold and tired, drained by what now appeared to be a useless expenditure of energy during the past twelve hours. "Yes," he said. "You better call in the Shore Patrol, Officer."

Silk moaned and rose to his feet, still clutching his middle. "Officer, this man just assaulted me. Name's Rubin Silk . . . I'm a . . . lawyer." He fished out a calling card and extended it.

"Sure, sir," the Irishman answered politely. "But you'll have to come with us and file charges."

"But I was only protecting myself when he turned on me. I'm a lawyer. I represent . . . What are you doing?"

A handcuff had been slipped neatly over Silk's right wrist. A moment later, its mate encircled Harry's left.

"Just a precaution, sir. Routine with us," said the Irishman with good humor. "Now, if you'll step this way, gentlemen . . ."

Shackled that way, they were turned over to the Shore Patrol. A quick radio call to Navy Operations and then they were all off together, the carryall slipping and sliding wildly through the slushy streets as the driver raced for the Navy base. But they didn't go into the base. Just over the causeway, the car pulled up opposite the guard shack at Gate One. Inside, Henry Hunter waited for them.

"There's hot coffee here," Hunter said as the handcuffs were removed. "You both look as though you could use a cup." He nodded curtly to Harry and smiled at the lawyer. "Name's Henry Hunter, Mr. Silk. Sorry about all this mix-up."

"At last, someone with authority. Mr. Hunter . . ." Silk extracted yet another card. He's like a magician with those cards, Harry thought—a never-ending stream. Silk glared at the two policemen. "Mr. Hunter, these oafs . . ." He was puffy with rage, his every word spaced with outraged dignity.

Hunter threw up a hand. "I'm sorry, Mr. Silk. I have no jurisdiction here." He smiled pleasantly. "My authority starts just inside this gate, I'm afraid. The civil authorities will be here in a moment. You'll have to give us a written statement. There are forms to fill out. I'm sure you know what's required better than I."

Silk looked at him slyly. "And what if I don't file charges against him?"

"That's impossible. We'll need your statement. I'm afraid we'll have to insist upon it. There's also a matter of that handgun you discharged." He looked thoughtfully at the hole in Silk's coat and lifted an eyebrow. "I'm sure you have a license for the gun—and the silencer. You'll have to explain all of that."

"Really! This is most maddening. I'm being treated like a common criminal."

"Yes, yes . . . Put all of that into your statement if you wish. Ah! Here's the good Sheriff now."

Hunter opened the door to let in a bulky older man. Silk rose to leave. "Before I go," he said with dignity, "I'd like to use your telephone."

Hunter managed to look sad. "Of course. You can use the Sheriff's when you get there. I'm afraid ours is not in working order."

"I see. Am I to understand that I'm under some sort of arrest? If so, I must remind you that under criminal jurisprudence, I'm entitled to one phone call."

"Mr. Silk, I have no authority to arrest you," explained Hunter. "You're a matter for the civil authorities. Go along, now. You can call from the Sheriff's office and you won't be bothered by anyone. Again, I apologize for all these formalities. St. John's the one we want."

When Silk had left, Hunter looked Harry over thoughtfully. He rubbed his jaw tenderly and asked, "Where did you learn to hit like that?"

"Some things you learn at boot camp you never forget."

"I don't mind saying you've given me a hell of a hard time, Commander. I was aboard *Pickering* last night when you slipped around us. Would you mind telling me what you thought you were doing out there?" Hunter smiled briefly. "As Hemingway once observed—no one knew what the leopard was seeking at that altitude."

"I was looking for Slattery and maybe another, on Block Island."

"And you didn't find them?"

"No."

"So right now you've nothing but a wild gleam in your eye. No proof?"

"No. No proof. Just a damned good hunch. Unless of course, you count Silk's performance this morning. He *was* trying to kill me when I hit him."

"I doubt he'd say so. He's got a good story. He confronts you; you swing on him; the gun goes off accidentally. He's articulate and convincing. No, Commander, you'll need more than that. And the boat—there's the matter of the boat. What did you do with it?"

When Harry told him, Hunter chuckled. "Perfect. I've had hell's own time from *Argonne*'s Captain. Your friend Perrelli wasn't very cooperative either."

"Perrelli?"

"We're waiting for him now. He was picked up right after your call."

"What for?"

"This may come as a surprise, Commander, but we've decided to back your hunch."

"I don't understand. I thought I was under arrest."

"You still are. It's only that you'll have a certain freedom of action during the next hour that should be interesting to observe. The Sheriff's phone has been disconnected, by the way, so there's no worry Silk will give the game away."

"I'm not sure I understand."

Hunter sighed. "Commander, if you recall Meek's place, the first floor consists of a main room leading off to the street, a smaller back room where the Foundation's accounts are kept, and a corridor that leads off through a back door to the alley beyond. There's an old-fashioned bead curtain covering the entrance to the back hall." Hunter held up a shining object. "I've gone to some trouble to have this key to the back door made, also to oil the hinges of that door. It's my intention to go in the back way and hide in the hall behind the curtain as you go in the front door. A few minutes later, we'll send in Perrelli. That should produce some interesting reactions. You aren't afraid, are you?"

"Afraid? No! I'm just confused. I thought . . ."

"Commander, I'm telling you that we plan to witness the little drama you seem so eager to stage." Hunter glanced out the window as a jeep skidded to a shuddering stop just outside the guard shack. "Ah! Here's your radarman. Come on, Commander, let's test your hunch!"

Twenty

The house seemed even more dilapidated than he had remembered. Its woebegone air suggested innocence—certainly not the headquarters of a sophisticated espionage apparatus. He climbed the rotting steps and stopped at Meek's doorway. The shades were drawn. A moment of panic: could the Foundation be closed because of the snow? Then he heard voices. He opened the door, the shop bell once again tinkling out his presence. The musty smell was sharply familiar.

Meek was having tea with a clergyman. He looked up, mildly surprised, at Harry's entrance, but gave no sign of recognition. Harry closed the door softly and waited for the clergyman to finish speaking.

"As I said, my dear Meek, ours is only a small movement over here so far. Certainly not enough to warrant more than one vicar. But we have hopes, my dear fellow. Yes, we have hopes." Then he realized he mustn't sound too enthusiastic. "However, at the present, while my flock is very much in harmony with your noble cause, there are embarrassing financial burdens thrust upon us. If you will permit a small play on words, in this cause, the meek shall not inherit the wealth." A watery little laugh was trapped between sips of tea, and the Vicar, overcome by his own wit, came up coughing.

"Excuse me for one moment, Vicar," said Meek. He turned to Harry. "I'm sorry, but the Foundation is closed today. The snow, you see. If you would care to take one of our brochures and come back tomorrow . . ." He turned up his palms and shrugged his shoulders, as if to indicate there was nothing further he could suggest.

Harry experienced a bitter wave of self-doubt. He had expected Meek to tip his hand in some way or other. However, if Meek was indeed alarmed by Harry's reappearance on his doorstep, he certainly didn't show it. Far from it. There was a totally unexpected comic-opera normalness about the dusty little room, the absurd little man clucking sympathetically as the Vicar explained the financial woes of his parish. It was totally unreal to link together this farce with the loss of the destroyer. Yet it all added up. It had to.

"I only came about Slattery's receipt," Harry blurted out.

Meek's hand froze in midair, hovering over the coughing clergyman. He turned back to Harry. A small nervous tic began to work in a corner of one eye.

"I don't know what you're talking about. In any case, we are *closed*. I'll be glad to see you tomorrow. We open at nine in the morning."

The Vicar stopped coughing long enough to make an apology. "I'm truly sorry, my dear Meek. I had no idea you weren't open today. There's no cause to turn the wheel of commerce on my account. I too can stop by tomorrow."

"Well, I can't," Harry said. "Slattery's lost his receipt for a large sum of money. He sent me to get another one. He wants it *today*."

The Vicar stared curiously at Harry. "I believe I've heard

that name recently," he mused. "And your face looks familiar."

"Duke Slattery was the commanding officer of the destroyer that was lost," Harry replied. "Before he left Newport, Slattery made a large contribution to the Foundation. He needs that receipt."

"But," pursued the Vicar, "I seem to recall that he was lost with the other unfortunate seamen in that tragic episode."

"Yes, but he was found last night."

The Vicar nodded and smiled knowingly. "Whose arm doth bind the restless wave," he quoted, missing altogether the fierce look of hatred that now contorted Meek's features. "The powers of the Almighty are wondrous to behold!"

Even Meek found this rather too much to digest. "I'm afraid the Foundation can't assist you or Commander Slattery today," he said with a hint of desperation. "My bookkeeper won't be in until tomorrow."

"Why, Mr. Meek, how forgetful you are. I can see your bookkeeper from here." The Vicar rose and stepped into the adjoining room. "My dear Meek, it will only take a moment to verify that contribution. Would you please bring your records, young man."

By the very unexpectedness of his movement, the Vicar succeeded in turning around the bookkeeper's swivel chair. Beneath a green eyeshade, the face of Dieter confronted Harry!

A surprising number of things occurred in the next few seconds. As Harry withdrew his revolver, the shop bell tinkled behind him. An instant later, he was knocked to the floor with stunning force by the explosive charge of Perrelli. "I'll kill that bastard," the radarman roared.

Enormously heavy in his body cast, he shot through the door with the force of a flying piston. Unhappily, as Harry fell, the revolver slipped from his grasp and slid the few feet between him and Meek. It took the latter only an instant to scoop up the weapon. As Harry got back on his feet, the business end of the revolver was pointed straight at him, and Meek gave every indication of knowing how to use it. Perrelli disengaged himself from the unconscious Dieter, sucking the bleeding knuckles of one hand with obvious relish as he joined Harry. The Vicar held up one hand, as though he were addressing his flock.

"Please, my dear Meek, remove that foul evilness from your person."

"Quiet, you fool," snapped Meek.

"Yes, Vicar, please shut up," Harry said. "I'm sorry that you blundered into this."

"But I don't understand," the churchman said. "Who are you, young man?"

"Who I am isn't important. All you need know is your favorite Foundation was actually a front for a neat little espionage operation. Your friend Meek ran things from ashore. When his bookkeeper wasn't bookkeeping, he was the Coxswain of the destroyer *Somerset*. He actually controlled the actions of the ship's Commanding Officer. The two of them have been pilfering U.S. coding devices for the past year. I can assure you that Meek won't hesitate to shoot us all if he has to. Meek, where is Slattery?"

"Far from here, that I can tell you. Mr. Slattery is the honored guest aboard a Soviet submarine now returning to home base. Mr. Slattery has finally been permitted to rejoin his family, now that his principal usefulness appears to be over."

"Is that how you forced him to do your work? You held his family captive?"

Meek smiled. "Mr. Slattery has some, shall we say, bizarre sexual habits. There's also a little matter of murder."

"Poor, desperate Duke Slattery," Harry said. "I'm glad Cutter finally let him off the hook."

"Cutter? Surely not the distinguished *Admiral* Cutter!" exclaimed the churchman.

"The very same," Harry replied; "the founding father of this worthy organization." He flipped open one of the Foundation's brochures, disclosing a picture of Cutter heading an eloquent testimony to the work of the organization. "A nice little game it was, too," he continued. "Cutter managed to have himself assigned as the officer in charge of the counterintelligence unit that was to uncover his own little espionage ring. What with his fame and his incessant speeches downgrading the fleet, the Navy was only too pleased to appoint him to an assignment that would take him out of the limelight. When the former Ship's Executive Officer threatened to give away the whole thing, Cutter had him drugged and thrown overboard. But even that was a near thing, and the ship was still under suspicion. Things were getting a bit out of hand, and Cutter decided that in order to save himself, he would have to eliminate the entire environment in which the operation was carried out. He personally selected me as the scapegoat."

"Rather a nice touch, don't you think?" Meek nodded pleasantly. "A two-time loser, as it were."

"Oh, dear me," the Vicar said. "It's hard to believe such evilness could exist in this world."

"You *are* a fool," Meek snapped. "But it occurs to me that your do-gooding can at last serve a useful purpose. I think we are now ready for the last artistic stroke to this canvas." He was interrupted by a low moan.

Dieter rose slowly to his feet. Once upright, he swayed slowly back and forth, his hand clasping his genitals. A gout of crimson blood pulsed from his broken nose and coursed down one corner of his cheek. Pure hatred shone in his yellow eyes. He lurched forward.

"No, no, Dieter. You can have your fun later," interrupted Meek. "I think the Newport police would not be too surprised if they found the Vicar in his church with a broken neck and next to him the body of our friend St. John. It would look as though the good Commander had sought sanctuary in the church, and not finding it, was forced to kill his reluctant host. Once he had done that, the only alternative for this desperate man, given the certainty of his eventual capture, would be suicide. If the Newport police are too obtuse to come to the same conclusion, I could perhaps assist in a modest way. Since we are closed for the day, Vicar, it would not be unnatural for me to call upon you—just as the last shot is fired in the vestry. Yes, I think it will all hold together nicely."

"Good Lord, surely you don't intend . . ." The Vicar's eyes bulged wih disbelief.

"I'm afraid he does, Vicar. You might as well save your breath." Harry turned back to Meek. "And what about Perrelli?"

"I rather think Dieter can find a way to dispose of him. He is not connected in any way with the collision. It may be some months before he's found. Just another of your sailors who saw fit to go over the hill, as I think it's called."

"That's quite good, Meek. And more than enough, I think. I hope you heard it all, Hunter. God knows I'll need your corroboration."

Henry Hunter stepped from behind the bead curtain. Meek whirled as the truncheon descended once, hard on his wrist. The pistol fell to the floor as Meek clutched his shattered wrist. With a snarl, Dieter leaped through the curtain and straight into the arms of two waiting Shore Patrolmen.

"You were wrong, Vicar," said Harry. "If you remember your quotations, think of the one that goes 'the meek, the terrible meek . . . about to enter their inheritance.' "

But the Vicar had long since fainted.

As a fiery sun broke over the eastern Mediterranean, the quartet of American destroyers slowed speed, the middle two veering outward from line-astern formation to positions on the flanks that gave the division a diamond configuration. Aboard the flagship, the Commodore slowly sipped steaming black coffee and pulled thoughtfully on his cigarette. He stared at the empty sea astern of his vessels with a puzzled expression. "Don't understand it," he said. "Navigator, are you *sure* this is our rendezvous position?"

The navigator, an ensign from Kansas who up until nine months ago had never even clapped eyes on a sextant, much less scaled the horizon with one, refused to be rattled by this bald reflection on his capabilities. As though touched on matters of navigation, the Commodore had asked this question of him a dozen times a day ever since they had sailed from Norfolk. "Yes, sir. I ran off the morning-star sights and checked them against the LORAN. This morning we had as good a horizon as I've ever had over here. This is one of the best morning fixes I've been able to get in some time." He knew what the next question would be and so got right to it. "It also checks with the dead-reckoning plot and fathometer readings."

"Then where the hell is that Russian destroyer?"

"Dunno, sir. I guess we outran him last night."

"But we doubled back. He could still have made the rendezvous if he knew where it was—and they always have before. I'm still not sure your fix is all that . . ."

As if to belie the Commodore's words, with a great frothing *whoosh* of compressed air a rusty black shape emerged from the sea a mile forward of the division flagship.

"Submarine! Dead ahead!" Both bridge lookouts screamed their discovery.

The submarine rose before them, dripping brine and trailing weeds like some predatory monster. A winking portable light on the slender sail flashed the identification signal.

"He's *Blackfish,* sir," the navigator said. He consulted his stopwatch and grinned slyly. "*His* navigation's pretty good too."

The radio speaker in the flagship's pilothouse crackled with the sound of UHF radio transmission. "*Blackfish* to Division Commander: Good morning! Ready to commence exercises."

The Commodore grabbed the phone. "Okay, *Blackfish,* but where the hell is that Russky that's been following us around? You seen him?"

"We lost him when we doubled back last night. I guess he didn't know our rendezvous position."

"Since when, *Blackfish*? Ivan's known it every time we've met before."

"Aye, sir. Must be a breakdown in their intelligence."

The Commodore's voice bristled with doubt. "Praise God from whom all blessings flow, eh? Well, maybe you're right. Let's hope it's a permanent breakdown."

Some two thousand miles away, the Lieutenant Commander standing on the edge of the runway at Prestwick, Scotland, and watching a Lockheed Orion intelligence-gathering aircraft settle gingerly to the ground said much the same thing to the squadron Operations Officer. "A whole new ball game" was the way he phrased it.

"Two sorties in a row and *no* MIGs?" asked the Operations Officer.

"Right. They're buzzing around out there looking for us, but now they don't seem to know when we start tracking. By the time their radar picks us up, we get a good twenty minutes for the run. When the MIGs finally show up, we head for the barn. Their fuel capacity won't permit them to chase us very far. *And* we have what we came for anyway. It's amazing! Something's sure happened."

"You think it was that last change in the Truxton Ciphers?"

"Changing that system never stopped them before. No, something's happened that I can't explain."

"For an intelligence officer, that's an interesting admission," the Operations Officer said with a grin.

The Air Intelligence Officer was right. Something had happened. All over the Atlantic, units of the Fleet found sea and air empty of the Russian snoopers that had harassed them constantly over the past few years. Getting rid of those troublesome pests was a strange and thoroughly pleasant experience.

"Oh, by the way, that Russian sub we tracked across the Atlantic has been scrubbed," continued the Intelligence Officer. "He dived just outside of Gibraltar. We'll try to pick him up on the seabed monitors. He'll probably stay under until he hits the Aegean, then on to the Black Sea, Odessa, vodka and caviar. I've passed him on to a destroyer division that's exercising off Crete with one of our subs. Might pick up some useful fingerprints."

However, the American destroyer division failed to make contact with this particular submarine returning from Yankee patrol. When the Russian captain picked up the screw beats of the Americans, he dived the big Y Class ballistic-missile boat deep under the thermolayer and detoured far south to avoid detection. He was content to bring the big submarine, with its sixteen two-stage Sawfly missiles, home without further adventures. It had been a difficult patrol, a cruise that demanded his best by day and night—especially that hair-raising approach to an American island to take aboard a top-secret V.I.P. in a snowstorm. Afterward, he had been only too glad to part company from his sister boat and run full out for home.

Duke Slattery's memory of that journey was mercifully foggy. He had fainted several times in the little rubber boat, until finally a deep protective coma settled over him during the painful journey down the submarine's ladder.

"Daw-bru-yeh oo-truh, Komrad Slattery."

Through the red ache of pain throbbing within him, he heard the submarine doctor's greeting. The words came back slowly, like a nightmare being replayed.

"Kahk-d'i lah?" The doctor smelled of fish and sweat. He wanted to know how Slattery felt.

"Hora," Slattery croaked. "Zhahr-kuh." The words came to him from the misty past. He knew only that he must tell the doctor about his leg.

The doctor grinned broadly. He had big yellow teeth, the upper incisors widely separated. He put his hand on Slattery's shoulder and said it was all right.

A corpsman appeared beside the doctor carrying a small mirror. In the glass Slattery could see the other half of the compartment: off-watch sailors stretched out on bunks exactly like his own, pipes crisscrossing through the compartment in insane spaghetti patterns, a myriad of valves and gauges, finally the bolted-down door to the next compartment. Somewhere behind him, someone began to play an accordion very softly. The corpsman, a young sailor with a soft, hairless chin, adjusted the mirror as the doctor gently pulled back the bedsheet. "Chood-nuh!" the doctor exclaimed, pleased with his own handiwork.

Slattery didn't answer him. He had to see. He had to look in the glass and see. He started up from the bunk, his movements strangely clumsy. The doctor let him look and then pinned him down. It didn't matter. The mirror confirmed what he feared must be so. His right leg now ended just before the knee.

Epilogue

Cutter had lived in mortal fear of this moment for most of the past year, but now that his time had come he felt unprepared yet strangely unafraid. The message, sent Immediate—Plain Language over Navy circuits, lay upon his otherwise empty desk top.

AS RESULT COMNAVBASE INVESTIGATION FOUNDATION AS OF NOON TODAY DETERMINED BANKRUPT AND FURTHER OPERATIONS WITH NAVAL ESTABLISHMENT NO LONGER POSSIBLE. ANTICIPATE FULL INVESTIGATION. HALLIDAY HANDCARRYING RECORDS FOR REVIEW BY CONTROLLER. WILL DELIVER 2000 TONIGHT. RECOMMEND ATTENDANCE BY CUTTER WITH WASHINGTON DOCUMENTATION. TRAVEL CHARGEABLE COMNAVBASE ALLOTMENT 78-110183; APPROPRIATION 478653. REQUEST ADVISE TRAVEL PLANS.

At this point the Admiral didn't know what had gone wrong, but he did know the outcome of the Newport affair. Controller was the code name for the Yankee Class submarine that was to take him off Montauk Point at eight o'clock that night—if he could get to it. However, for some strange reason it no longer seemed to matter to him. On the contrary, it now seemed as though an enormous weight had been lifted from his shoulders. Even when the sound of angry voices in his outer office reached him a few moments later, he refused to allow himself the luxury of the sensation of fear. He simply rose, placed his cap square upon his head, and marched out the side door of his office, as he had done countless times before in answering unexpected summonses to the White House or to the Hill. There was no one watching the side exit, and he merged quickly into the stream of traffic in the corridor. However, as his taxi pulled away from the loading ramp, he could hear alarmed cries and the pounding of feet just behind him. He smiled to himself, and lit one of his aromatic cigars.

Thirty minutes later, the taxi deposited him at the intersection of Calvert Street and Connecticut Avenue. He fished out a ten-dollar bill, and to the astonishment of the taxi driver, without waiting for change he sauntered casually back over the bridge in the direction of the exclusive Kalorama section: an elderly man, distinguished and successful, wafting perfumed cigar smoke upon the early-spring afternoon. He heard the screech of brakes behind him and was aware of the gray Navy sedan as it roared up the bridge to take a position blocking traffic ahead of him. But it did not matter, he thought, as he stopped midway across the bridge.

One step from appointment as Chief of Naval Operations, he had just failed to bring it off—the end of an otherwise illustrious career. He wondered how future generations would judge him. He leaned over the bridge and looked down: A five-hundred-foot drop to the roadway below—sure and certain, once he released his grip. No stomach pump could save him. Surgery that could sometimes repair the damage caused by a misplaced bullet could never repair the damage of that flight. An unemotional man, he was astonished to discover tears coursing down his cheeks. He watched the wet end of his cigar float lazily earthward. So this was how it was to finish. Chief of Naval Operations, the Joint Chiefs of Staffs, perhaps then the Senate, even the White House—all these dreams gone because of one mistake years ago and a foolish girl who had tried to save him. His great talents, his vast experience, his brilliance, all wasted.

Suddenly he couldn't do it. Once the President heard, once the Senate listened . . . He backed off from the bridge railing.

A moment before, in the jeep, the Shore Patrol officer had cried, "My God, He's going to jump! Drive like hell, up the curb. I'll try and grab him." The jeep jumped up on the sidewalk as Cutter stepped back. There was a soft thump and a shriek of tortured metal as the jeep ricocheted off the concrete wall of the bridge. Cutter, still conscious, was catapulted forward, up and over the railing. For an instant he hung suspended on the bridge railing; then he slid slowly forward, headfirst, into the traffic stream that snaked homeward so very far below. "Oh, my God," moaned the youngster who drove the jeep. Oblivious of his torn, bloody scalp, the realization dawned upon him that he had just killed an admiral.

"I just want to know *why* you did it."

"Why are we what we are?"

Harry shook his head. "That's not good enough, Diane. Was it Cutter? Did he force you into this? We don't have much time if I'm going to help you."

The brig had not been built so as to accommodate both sexes. She was to be taken that morning to the naval prison at Portsmouth, New Hampshire. He would not see her again.

"Hairbreadth Harry to the rescue of his little Nell?" She laughed bitterly. "It may be a shock, my dear, but I've been in this for years. I'm surprised I wasn't caught long before."

"But your family, your upbringing . . ."

"Not the sort of background"—she glanced around—"for this?"

"It was Cutter, wasn't it?"

"Oh, yes, it *was* Cutter. But not in the way you think. You don't know him. For once the Pentagon cookie cutter turned out a man not just brilliant, but compassionate as well.

"He didn't have to warn that convoy. And he didn't have to cover for his commodore. If the Commodore had lived, he would have taken the weight from Christian's shoulders." She shook her head in wonderment. "Eight weeks at sea, out of touch with the world. Well, he did it. He saved that ship and what was left of the crew. He saved the convoy, too. They gave him the Navy Cross for it. Read the citation sometime. What would you have done? Blame your dead commodore for something neither one of you had the authority to do? What good would it have done? They'd already made a routine change in the code.

"After the war, he took care of my mother; he saw me through school. He kept us together. What did you want me to do when Meek threatened to expose him—the receipt, the old code, photographs, the lot? Of course I had to save him. Wouldn't you? He was in a box, an awful box."

Suddenly he asked, "Diane, who was your father? I mean, your *real* father."

"Don't you know by now? Haven't you guessed? I told you I came from a Navy family. My father was Commodore Halliday, the man who asked his Flag Captain to do something reprehensible to both of them and then, knowing he was dying, made that officer promise to look after his own family. You're the Nelson type. I ask you, would Hardy have done less?"

She turned toward him, not altogether in control of herself—her hands strangely fragile within the cruel manacles; her uniform jacket slung across her shoulder giving her the look of a thin, handsome hussar. "People are all that count in this world," she said softly. "He was kind, gentle, and honorable—yes, honorable. I *had* to help him. Don't you see?"

"That afternoon in your apartment when we made love. That was to make me forget the Tuinal, wasn't it? When you found I'd discovered it, you had to do something to stop me from asking questions—to make me forget. Wasn't that it?"

"I won't answer any more questions. Go away."

"Just answer that last one," he said, his voice harsh.

"Go away!" She retreated to a corner of the cell.

"Answer me!"

"What do you want me to say? That I cared for you? Of course I did. But what good could ever come of it? I was finished when we first met. Go away!"

He left her then.

The noisy thumpings of a military band reached him faintly through the open window. He glanced away from MacDonald and saw in the roadstead a division of destroyers returning to berth. The band, the crowd at the pier, and the battered, lean look of the vessels told him the division had been at sea a long time—perhaps Vietnam, more likely the Mediterranean. Outside . . . outside was life. Inside—well, this room could hold nothing but painful memories for him. He drummed his fingers restlessly on the table and studied MacDonald.

"This is, of course, highly irregular, Lieutenant Hunter," the old man said. "On the other hand, this entire case has been highly irregular."

"Most irregular," echoed Hawk peevishly.

Hunter smiled and rubbed his discolored jaw. "With the court's permission, I wonder if the witness would like to tell us when he first knew Slattery had escaped the collision."

"During the testimony of *Argonne*'s Commanding Officer," Harry explained. "I knew I had seen *Somerset*'s whaleboat in the water that night. A whaleboat can't disappear, and if you recall the testimony, it was made very clear that the boat wasn't recovered."

"And you say you had been drugged when all of this happened?" MacDonald asked.

"That's right, sir. A common prescription sleeping pill, powdered and slipped into my coffee. I imagine James was also—and Abel, for that matter."

"You believe Abel was murdered, then," Hunter asked.

"Oh, I'm certain of it. I think he had been driven to the brink of insanity by Slattery and Dieter. Then he tumbled to what was going on and had to be disposed of. It was just good luck on O.N.I.'s part that he happened to have that rotor in his pocket. I'm sure Dieter will confirm that supposition."

"Yes, it was lucky," mused Burnside. "And the money?"

"I think I can answer that, sir," interjected Hunter. "The other side is not as generously endowed, shall we say, as similar U.S. activities. Slattery was desperate. He needed that money.

"Actually, that's what first alerted us in Counterintelligence. Up till then, Cutter had his own way. He even persuaded the brass to put him in charge of the special project investigating the leak in the Truxton Ciphers. The Navy was glad to do it. Sideline him for a bit. He was, of course, desperate for that assignment. Who would ever suspect the man in charge of the investigation as the man responsible for the espionage in the first place?

"It was just luck that the auditors did a routine check-out of *Somerset*'s accounts after the collision and accidentally reported their findings to O.N.I. Counterintelligence instead of Cutter's Special Project Office. Then when we found out about James's death as well as Abel and the missing rotor, we began to put things together. Usual bureaucratic foul-up that brought us into the picture in the first place. If the auditors had been following directives, they would have reported directly to Cutter's office."

"No foul-up, Lieutenant," said Harry. "I'd like to think it was Fate."

"Anyway," Hunter continued, "wherever Slattery is now, I'm sure he'll find a use for that money, if his superiors let him keep it. I suspect they won't."

"The Russians had a hold on Slattery?" Hawk asked.

"The shrinks tell me Slattery was a sadist. Apparently he exploded in Russia during the war and accidentally killed a girl. One-way mirrors, the whole thing on film, usual Russian heavy-handedness . . . you can put it together."

"Then those *graffiti* in the Crypto shack?"

"Commander, that was probably Slattery and not Abel, as I gather you surmised."

"And when Dieter tried to get me lost in the boat?"

"He may have been trying to kill you then. Fake a break-down, send the crew for help, the two of you alone in the fog." Hunter smiled coolly. "You were just lucky. Not so Ted James. They got very nervous when James was ordered aboard. They didn't understand that Cutter had to protect himself, make it all look good. They knew James worked for Cutter, and they thought the Admiral was going to double-cross them."

"Why would Dieter want to kill me in the whaleboat? After all, the code had been changed, so the missing rotors wouldn't affect *Somerset* at all."

"Yes. Cutter ordered the code rotation right after the girl told him what you had discovered. How he must have cursed Slattery and Dieter's carelessness! But you see, Dieter didn't know the code was changed. I think he thought you were going ashore to report the missing rotors."

"Sure, it fits now," said Harry. "That's why Slattery shot

off that message transferring responsibility for the coding devices to me. He wiped his own slate clean in case there'd been an investigation."

"That's right. Having nailed you with the responsibility, they began looking for ways to put you on the sideline. I think the hangfire was Slattery's idea, although Dieter would have been the one to work it out. Keep you off balance like Abel, maybe physically harm you so you wouldn't be in the way. When did you tumble to the girl?"

"It was all so obvious I missed it for a long, long time," Harry replied miserably. "Remember, Cutter directed me to her in Newport. If I hadn't met her, she'd probably have arranged to meet me. I was splendidly under control, both ashore and afloat." He shook his head ruefully.

"And of course, the sleeping pills she had to get for Slattery. They couldn't chance a medic reporting a prescription of sleeping pills for the Commander of a Navy ship on operational duty." He could have added that he had slept with the girl and she obviously didn't need pills. "But the pills were a mistake. They should have used Dieter or Meek for that. According to Jacoby, she had that prescription refilled just before the ship sailed, and that bottle was half full the last time I saw it.

"But the real clincher for me was my note. If I had actually caught up with Dieter and Slattery, I'd have needed all the help I could get. On the other hand, they were reasonably certain I'd be caught, and without that note to back up my story, it would look as though I had dreamed up the wildest possible explanation after being caught. The note was the clincher. Considering our relationship, there was no other explanation for her behavior." It hurt him to talk about her like that, and he looked away.

Hawk spoke up. "Lieutenant Hunter, I find it very difficult to believe that Admiral Cutter could have done anything so foolish as to give away those codes to the Soviet in 1942."

"Then you'll have to see the contents of Meek's safe. We have the old codes themselves, the receipt Cutter foolishly countersigned, and some interesting photography. We dug up an old *Jane's Fighting Ships,* and from what our experts tell us, it looks as though he's aboard the *Vorovsky,* a relic of the Czarist Navy."

"But why did he have to give them the code?"

"You can see his ship in the background—an old four-piper. I'm no sea dog, but one look at that ship and I'd have said she wouldn't last another thirty minutes. Night coming on. A convoy to warn. Maybe an hour to get off the message that had to be coded. Our convoys had firm orders to disregard plain-language traffic. Too many inventive submariners in the German Navy. Anyway, another several hours to wait for the authentication request from the convoy. We were slow in those days. A sinking ship; no other officers left except a dying, desperate commodore. I don't know. What would you have done?"

"But the Russians? Didn't we have a joint U.S.–Russian code we could use in those days?"

"What do you do if the Russians say they don't carry it? And of course, if you had it, you would have carried it up on the bridge for instant use in the event you ran into a Soviet naval vessel. I'll show you the photo of Cutter's four-piper. There's nothing left of the bridge."

"Couldn't he have stayed aboard the Russian ship?"

"Sure—but if that four-piper with her remaining fifty men was going to make it to Archangel, then every second counted. The Russians were smart. They knew that. And they knew Cutter was a damned young captain. Annapolis ring, all that—a man who would go far if he survived the war. All they had to do was wait while he climbed up the ladder of success."

"Lieutenant," Harry said admiringly, "I just wish I had known about you sooner."

"How do you think *I* feel?" Hunter rubbed his discolored jaw and grinned painfully.

"Speaking for the Judge Advocate, I'd say the Navy was pretty lucky to have the two of you," Hawk said gently.

"Yes," agreed MacDonald. "I think we can declare this court of inquiry closed. St. John, I have been instructed to send you straight back to Washington." He smiled mysteriously. "The Chief told me on the phone this morning he has a small token of the Navy's appreciation to personally give to you."

They were all smiling at him now. "Go ahead, Davy, tell him the rest," pressed Hawk.

"Well, I think that had better be revealed by the Chief himself. However, I can say you are due for a new set of shoulder boards. Also, you might start looking over the list of this new destroyer construction that's going on. I'm told good commanding officers are getting harder to find."

Outside the War College, Harry paused before getting into the sedan. The crowd of activists and idlers had dispersed, presumably bent on some new crusade. The sun shone warmly upon him. On the meticulous lawn, a small patch of clover poked through the warming soil. He bent down and picked one of the small plants from the ground.

"Harry, please hurry," begged Pozo. "I have to put you both on a plane."

"Both?"

A familiar face appeared in the back of the car. "Hiyuh, Commander. I guess we're both heroes. Wait'll those Washington birds find out the Spider's coming to town." Perrelli snapped his fingers and rolled his eyes heavenward. "Let the good times roll."

"Don't book any dates for a while, sailor." Harry grinned. "There's still a matter of public brawling to be settled."

"Aw, Commander . . ."

"Your only way out, Perrelli, is to ship over as my Chief Radarman."

"Hey, Commander."

"Harry, will you hurry up!" Pozo complained.

But before he got into the car, *Somerset*'s Executive Officer paused one last time. "May God hold you in the palm of his hand," he said. Softly he blew the small plant from his fingers so that its flight was north, the direction of New Hampshire. Then he climbed into the car.